CHICKEN RUN

CHICKEN RUN

Adapted from the screenplay by Ellen Weiss
Screenplay by Karey Kirkpatrick
Story by Peter Lord and Nick Park
Directed by Peter Lord and Nick Park
Produced by Peter Lord, David Sproxton, and Nick Park

CHICKEN RUN

PUFFIN BOOKS

Published by the Penguin Group

Penguin Putnam Books for Young Readers, 345 Hudson Street,
New York, New York 10014, U.S.A.

Penguin Books Ltd, 27 Wrights Lane, London W8 5TZ, England

Penguin Books Australia Ltd, Ringwood, Victoria, Australia

Penguin Books Canada Ltd, 10 Alcorn Avenue, Toronto, Ontario, Canada M4V 3B2

Penguin Books (N.Z.) Ltd, 182–190 Wairau Road, Auckland 10, New Zealand

Penguin Books Ltd, Registered Offices: Harmondsworth, Middlesex, England

Published by Puffin Books,
a division of Penguin Putnam Books for Young Readers, 2000

3 5 7 9 10 8 6 4 2

Puffin Books ISBN 0-14-130875-3

Printed in the United States of America

Table of Contents

Chapter 1

The Escaping Game

The full moon shone down on the rolling English countryside, casting its brilliant light on the serene beauty of the Yorkshire Dales. Everything looked untroubled, peaceful.

Except for the chain-link fence.

The lovely countryside came to a screeching halt at the fence. Topped with barbed wire, the fence surrounded an ugly, dusty yard in which sat several squat rows of huts. Under the pale moonlight, the place looked a bit like a wartime prison camp, but on an oddly smaller scale.

A flashlight threw its beam this way and that among the huts. It was held by an oafish-looking, pot-bellied man. The man was making his evening rounds, checking the perimeter of the yard, accompanied by two large, menacing guard dogs. The dogs had metal spikes sticking out of their collars.

After checking the huge padlock on the gate, the man moved on.

When he had gone, a silhouetted figure emerged from behind one of the huts. The figure ran from one corner of a hut to another. It was a chicken. Her name was Ginger.

Stealthily, Ginger dashed across the yard to the fence. She leaned against the fence for a moment, breathing hard, and then produced a spoon. After a few minutes of digging madly, she had made a hole at the base of the fence. She scrambled under the fence and dashed for the cover of a building, leaping behind it just as the flashlight beam panned past.

Whew. Safe. She looked back toward the hut inside the fence and gave the okay sign to five other chickens who were anxiously waiting there, heads poking out from behind the hut. Scampering to the fence, they tried to crawl under.

Unfortunately, the largest hen, whose name was Bunty, found herself wedged halfway through. She was too big to make it.

"I'm stuck!" squawked Bunty.

Her friend Babs, with help from the others, now tried pushing from behind. Ginger hurried over and pulled from the front. Bunty was struggling frantically, beginning to panic.

Suddenly—*uh-oh!* A light, shining on Ginger!

"Get back!" Ginger whispered to the others. But it was

too late for Ginger. The farmer was already siccing the barking, lunging dogs on her.

Ginger shoved Bunty back and then ran for her life. Another dog rounded the corner and joined the others, charging her. She ran up the steps of the farmhouse and backed toward the door as the dogs stalked her, snarling. Then, suddenly—

The farmhouse door opened, instantly causing the dogs to stop snarling and cower in terror. Ginger spun around to find herself staring into the heart-stopping face of . . . *the dreaded Mrs. Tweedy.* Mrs. Tweedy, scourge of the chicken farm, bringer of misery.

Even though the farm had been in Mr. Tweedy's family for generations, it was Mrs. Tweedy who really wore the pants there, and all the animals knew it. Her husband simply did her bidding and tried to stay out of trouble. Ginger might have felt sorry for him if he weren't such a great spineless lump.

"Mr. Tweedy!" she demanded of her husband. "What is that chicken doing *outside* the fence?"

"Dunno, luv," Mr. Tweedy stammered. "I, I, I . . ."

"Just deal with it. Now!" barked Mrs. Tweedy.

"Yes, luv."

BLAM! Mrs. Tweedy slammed the door.

Mr. Tweedy scowled at Ginger, the source of his present misery. Once again, for the hundredth time, or perhaps the thousandth, she'd made him look stupid. Well, could

Ginger help it if he *was* stupid?

Without a word, Mr. Tweedy scooped her up and carried her across the dusty yard, to an old coal bunker near the side of the barn. "I'll teach you to make a fool of me," he muttered as he trudged along.

He threw her inside the bunker, slammed it closed, and then marched over to the fence. "Let that be a lesson to the lot of you!" he shouted through it at the rest of the chickens. "*No chicken escapes from Tweedy's farm!*"

Mr. Tweedy turned on his heel and marched back to the house.

And that was that—just another bad day for chickens at Tweedy's Farm. Just another round in the endless, depressing game: Chickens Try to Escape, Chickens Get Caught.

In the gloom of the coal bunker, Ginger marked off the days on the wall. She knew just what was happening to her friends outside. It was always the same. They sat cramped on their little nests in the chicken huts, prisoners to the relentless pressure to produce more eggs. And the pressure had gotten worse lately. Mrs. Tweedy had been walking around with charts and graphs, and the graphs showed that the egg yield was declining. Mrs. Tweedy was not happy. Of course, Mrs. Tweedy was never happy, but these days she appeared to be in an even more unpleasant state than usual. In the darkness of the coal bunker, Ginger worried about what it all meant.

Finally, Mr. Tweedy let Ginger out of the bunker, as he always did sooner or later. The blinding sun made her squint, but she had no time to adjust to the light, because Mr. Tweedy was already scooting her toward the yard and booting her inside the gate.

The coal bunker had just been a slight interruption in Ginger's campaign to break out of Tweedy's. It wasn't fun to be in there, but as many times as she was thrown into it, the bunker never broke her will. Time and time again, Ginger went to the coal bunker. And time and time again she returned to the huts, ready to try another plan. Ginger was going to get them all out, even if she had to go to the coal bunker a million times.

Now, with Ginger back home, the plotting could begin again. Elaborate escape plans were immediately spread out on a makeshift table in Hut 17, which was Escape Central, the nerve center of the chicken farm.

Ginger's right-hand hen was the bespectacled Mac, the engineer of the group. It was Scottish Mac who could be relied on to come up with the technical know-how to execute all their escape plans. If valiant Ginger was the heart of the outfit, Mac was the brains.

Then there was big, hardy, plain-spoken Bunty, and beside her the sweet but dotty Babs, always knitting placidly away. These chickens formed the core of Ginger's hen-house family, and they were all willing to throw themselves into Ginger's endless escape schemes, no matter how perilous they turned out to be.

And so, the next time Mr. Tweedy wheeled the egg cart out through the open gate, something unusual was taking place behind him in the chicken yard. Unseen by him, a small chicken-feeding trough rose up on a pair of chicken feet and dashed for the gate. It wedged itself into the gate to keep it from closing. A moment later, behind it, a much larger feeding trough rose up, this one on *several* pairs of chicken feet. The big feeder lurched across the yard, hit the gate sideways, and panicked. Finally it tipped over. Mr. Tweedy looked back to find out what the ruckus was, and saw many pairs of upside-down chicken feet, trying to run in midair.

Back to the coal bunker for Ginger, for more days and nights of waiting and plotting in the dark.

And then, out again and on to the next secret escape plan: a tunnel dug into the floor of the henhouse. The tunnel had been painstakingly dug with spoons, inch by inch, while Mr. Tweedy was occupied elsewhere. All the chickens had taken turns digging. Ginger, naturally, was the first to try it out. She was lowered into the tunnel, where she lay down on a waiting roller skate. Then, *zoom*—through the tunnel and up to the surface, where she madly cranked an eggbeater to break through the surface.

Ginger was free! She popped up through the hole, looked around, climbed out.

And bumped right into a snarling, slobbering, growling dog. Oops. There'd been a slight miscalculation about where to come up on the far end.

Back to the coal bunker. Back to marking off the days on the wall.

And… back out again.

This time, an odd-looking version of Mrs. Tweedy, with long, awkward stick legs and arms, was seen lumbering through the gate and past the dogs. This rather confused the dogs: it *looked* like their mistress, but *was* it their mistress? It didn't *smell* like their mistress. …

Suddenly the hem of the dress caught on a wheelbarrow. The dress slid off the strange form, revealing … chickens. Quite a few chickens. They were standing on each other's shoulders, busily operating the sticks and levers that moved the dummy Mrs. Tweedy.

The dogs were no longer confused. They charged, and the chickens scurried back into the yard.

This time, the lid to the coal bunker slammed behind Ginger with a bang that seemed to reverberate forever and ever.

It's All in Your Head, Mr. Tweedy

The sun rose on the compound. Fowler, the chicken yard's lone rooster, shuffled to the edge of the rooftop, leaned heavily on his walking stick, cleared his throat, and crowed.

"Company! Fall in!" he ordered in a cracked voice. He wasn't as young as he had been, but he still tried to sound as military as possible. After all, he had his dignity. He had tradition to uphold. It wasn't everybody who had been a member of the Royal Air Force.

In the coal bunker, Ginger sat bouncing a turnip against the wall, just waiting out her time. At last, the door opened and out she came.

Mr. Tweedy led Ginger over to the fence and booted her through the gate. She landed on her face in front of her compatriots.

"Morning, Ginger," said Babs pleasantly. "Back from

holiday?" Poor Babs. A good soul, she was, good as gold, but not the sharpest knife in the drawer.

"I wasn't on holiday, Babs," Ginger explained, not for the first time. "I was in solitary confinement."

"Awwww," clucked Babs, "it's nice to get a bit of time to yourself, isn't it?"

Ginger shook her head. No matter how many times she tried to explain, Babs couldn't seem to understand. And why upset her, anyway? Best to leave it alone.

Just then, a bell rang loudly. Instantly, the chickens sprang into panic-stricken action, pouring frantically out of their huts.

Along came Fowler. He stationed himself in front of the nervous chickens as they fell into formation.

"Roll call!" he barked. "Pip, pip, quick march, what-what!"

Ginger and Babs hurried to join the line. Babs hid her knitting as Fowler marched down the line, looking crotchety.

"Come along, chaps, this is no time for dawdling. Why, back in my RAF days, when the senior officer called for a scramble, you'd hop in the old crate and tallyho! Chocks away!"

He continued crankily down the line until he arrived at Bunty, who was the biggest hen. Bunty was not having any of it. "Aw, give over, you old fool," she groused. "They just want to count us."

"How dare you talk back to a senior ranking officer," Fowler huffed. "Why, back in my RAF days..."

"Fowler, they're coming," Ginger hissed. "Back in line."

Fowler hopped into the line. "Right. Atten-*tion!*" he ordered one last time. To Bunty, he said, "There'll be a stern reprimand for you, lad. You're grounded!"

Now the chickens really did snap to attention, because the Tweedys were entering the yard. Mr. Tweedy was pushing the egg cart, while Mrs. Tweedy marched down the line like a camp commandant.

Beside Ginger stood the ever-alert Mac. "Welcome back, hen," said Mac softly. "Is there a new plan?"

Keeping a watchful eye trained on Mrs. Tweedy, Ginger secretly slipped Mac a folded scrap of paper. Mac discreetly unfolded it, peered through her glasses, and examined it. She looked confused. "I thought we tried going under," she whispered.

Ginger quickly reached over and flipped the drawing right side up.

"Ah," said Mac. "Over. Right."

At the same time Ginger had been handing Mac the new plans, Mr. Tweedy had handed Mrs. Tweedy a clipboard. She scanned it, her face expressionless as usual.

"How's the egg count?" Ginger asked anxiously.

"I laid five this morning," reported Bunty. She puffed out her chest and beamed proudly. "Five! Well chuffed with that, I was. Well chuffed."

"Quiet in the ranks," muttered Fowler under his breath.

"What about everyone else . . . ?" Ginger started asking, ignoring Fowler.

But Mrs. Tweedy had now lowered the clipboard and was casting an icy stare in the direction of a certain unlucky chicken named Edwina. The other chickens shuffled nervously and whispered among themselves.

"Oh no," moaned Ginger. "Edwina. Bunty, why didn't you give her some of your eggs?"

"I would have," Bunty replied in agony. "She didn't tell me, she didn't tell anyone!"

Mrs. Tweedy snapped her fingers and pointed to Edwina. In a flash, Mr. Tweedy grabbed her by the neck and carried her out through the gate, with Mrs. Tweedy following.

"Is Edwina off on holiday?" inquired the clueless Babs. She smiled and blinked dottily.

Poor Babs. She wasn't bright, but sometimes she was truly dim. Ginger couldn't bear to tell her that Mrs. Tweedy was not taking Edwina off on anything like a holiday.

Ginger had to see what happening to Edwina. Quickly, she climbed onto the roof of a hut in the far corner, just in time to see Mr. Tweedy carrying Edwina into—*eeeeek*!— the slaughter hut, just beside Mrs. Tweedy's office.

Ginger saw the door open. There was an ax leaning against the wall. She gasped, reflexively feeling her neck.

Now Mrs. Tweedy was entering the room, pulling on her red rubber gloves. In the half-light of the hut, frightening shadows were cast onto the wall. Mr. Tweedy placed Edwina on the chopping block. Mrs. Tweedy raised the ax and then began bringing it down.

Ginger turned away, but she couldn't escape the sound.

In the yard, the chickens shuffled and clucked nervously. Ginger, on the roof, bowed her head. In a moment, it was all over.

There was a squawk overhead. Ginger looked up to see a flock of geese winging their way across the sky. She followed them with her eyes as they flew toward a particularly lush hill in the distance. A beam of sunlight shone down on the geese, lighting them with an ethereal glow.

"We've got to get out of here," Ginger said to herself, staring at them as they receded into the distance.

"Ginger?"

It was Mac, standing on the ground below and calling up to her. Mac tapped the paper Ginger had given her. "Are we still on?" she asked.

Ginger screwed up her face, even more determined than ever. "Oh, we're on all right," she said. She gave Mac the thumbs-up. "Spread the word," she added. "Meeting tonight in Hut 17."

That night, three chickens could be seen darting across the open space toward the door of Hut 17. When they reached the door, they gave a secret knock.

A peephole popped open. Eyes peered out. The peephole closed. Then the door opened, the chickens slipped in, and the door quickly closed.

A minute later, there was another knock at the door. The peephole opened again. The eyes peered out again, but saw nothing until they looked down. Standing outside the door was a pair of rats. They looked like traveling salesmen, a little on the seedy side.

"You called?" asked one. "Nick—"

"And Fetcher," added the other.

"At your service," Nick concluded.

The door opened just enough to let Ginger slip out. It was she who had summoned the pair. Ginger moved furtively over to the side of the hut, keeping a wary eye on the farmhouse, where Mr. Tweedy was squinting out through the curtains.

"Over here," said Ginger quietly. "We need some more things."

"Right you are, Miss."

Whht-whht-whht! In three quick moves, the rats whipped out their briefcase, unfolded the legs, and lifted the top. They were open for business.

Nick pulled out a thimble. "How 'bout this quality hand-crafted tea set?" he offered.

Fetcher pulled out a bathtub stopper and chain. "Or this lovely necklace and pendant?" he said.

"Uh, no..." said Ginger.

Not to be outdone, Nick pulled out a badminton shuttlecock. "Or this beau'iful little number, all the rage in the fashionable chicken coops of Paris," he said. "Simply pop it on like so, and as the French hens say—*voila!*"

"That's French," Fetcher explained helpfully as he put the shuttlecock on Ginger's head.

"That's two hats in one, Miss," Nick continued. "For parties." He turned it upside down. "For weddings!" he said triumphantly.

"*For*-get it!" Ginger impatiently removed the "hat" and showed the rats the drawing she had given Mac earlier. "We're making this." Then she pointed to a list. "We need *these* things. Can you get them?"

"Ooh, this is a big job, Miss," said Nick, studying the list. "It's gonna cost."

"Same as always" said Ginger. "One bag of chicken feed ... "

"You call this pay?" Nick said.

"It's chicken feed," Fetcher added.

"What else could we give you?" Ginger asked, exasperated.

"Eggs," said Fetcher.

Ginger was horrified. "*Eggs*!?" It came out louder than she'd intended it to. She looked toward the farmhouse and lowered her voice. "We can't give you our eggs, they're too valuable."

Nick, unmoved, began packing up his case. "And so are we," he said, turning to leave. "After you, Fetcher."

"After I what?" said Fetcher, ever quick on the uptake.
"*Move!*" Nick barked at him.

Inside Mrs. Tweedy's office, Mr. Tweedy squinted out the window. He lifted a pair of binoculars to his eyes and continued stare as he absently chewed on a chicken drumstick. The leftover carcass of a roast chicken sat on a platter on the dinner table. Mrs. Tweedy, seated at her corner desk, was feverishly entering numbers on her hand-cranked adding machine.

"Fourteen shillings and thruppence," she muttered to herself. "Seven and sixpence . . . two and nine . . . fourpence ha'penny . . . *Ugh!*" She slammed her fist down and looked at the figures once more. Then she issued a frustrated sigh. "Stupid, worthless creatures," she said. "I'm sick and tired of making minuscule profits."

She glanced down to the pile of mail on her desk, where, as it happened, there was a magazine right on top. The headline read, "Sick and Tired of Making Minuscule Profits?"

Mrs. Tweedy picked up the magazine. The rest of the headline read, "Turn Your Chicken Farm into a Gold Mine." She stared hard at the words, the gears in her head almost visibly spinning. "Hmmm . . ." she said.

Mr. Tweedy, oblivious to this momentous "hmmm," continued to stare out the window. "Those chickens are up to summat," he said ponderously.

"Quiet," said his wife. "I'm onto something."

"They're organized," said Mr. Tweedy. "I know it." He was convinced: the chickens were plotting and planning, trying to make a fool of him.

"I said—*quiet.*"

Mr. Tweedy took that to mean he should whisper. "That ginger one—I reckon she's their leader."

Mrs. Tweedy slammed her magazine down, causing Mr. Tweedy to jump. "Mr. Tweedy!" she barked. Then she rose from her chair and slowly walked toward him, causing him to cower. "I may have found a way to finally make us some real money around here," she continued, "and what are you on about? Ridiculous notions of escaping chickens."

"B-b-but . . ."

She was right upon him now. "It's *all in your head*, Mr. Tweedy. Say it!" she yelled.

Mr. Tweedy was vanquished. "It's all in me head, it's all in me head . . ." he repeated dully.

"Now you keep telling yourself that," said Mrs. Tweedy, "because I don't want to hear another word about it. Is that clear?"

There was a pause as Mr. Tweedy considered it, and found that he could not resist just one more attempt. "But the ginger one, luv—"

"*They're chickens, you dolt!* Apart from you, they're the most stupid creatures on this planet! They don't plot, they don't scheme, and they are not *organized!*"

And that was that.

Here Comes Rocky

In Hut 17, Ginger ineffectually banged a makeshift gavel on a heater vent pipe. "Order, ORDER!" she yelled in frustration as the not-very-organized chickens continued to cluck and squawk softly among themselves. "Calm down, everyone!"

The room was filled with escape plan paraphernalia: drawings of past escape attempts with big X's through them, models, diagrams, charts, and even a pull-down, retractable map of the farmyard.

Fowler used his British military lung-power to help Ginger establish order. "*Quiet there!*" he shouted. "*Let's have some discipline in the ranks, what-what!*"

Everyone quieted down from the sheer volume of his command. "Thank you, Fowler," said Ginger.

"In my RAF days, we were never allowed to waste time with unnecessary chitchat," said Fowler with satisfaction.

"Yes, *thank you*, Fowler—"

Fowler suddenly noticed with a start that the hens had already settled down. "Right," he said, looking a little lost. "Carry on."

Ginger turned back to the others. "Now—our last escape attempt was a bit of a fiasco. But Mac and I have come up with a brand-new plan." She turned to Mac. "Show 'em, Mac," she said.

Mac set a model catapult on the table. "Right," she said in her no-nonsense Scottish accent. "We've tried going *under* the wire and that didnae work. So, the plan is—we go over it." She placed a turnip in the catapult. "This is us, right? We get in like this, wind her up, and let 'er go!"

Thoing! The turnip went flying and splatted against the wall above Fowler's head. The chickens gasped.

"Good grief!" said Fowler. "The turnip's bought it!" The chickens bawked and squawked and clucked in alarm.

Suddenly, the lookout chicken who was stationed at the window sat up. "Farmer's coming!" she cried.

Quick as a wink, they leaped into Operation Cover-up, a drill that had been rehearsed countless times. Bunks were moved, drawings hidden, the retractable map retracted. After ten seconds of intense scrambling, they all settled into their nests, looking blank and brainless.

The hinged top of the chicken hut lifted open, and Mr. Tweedy's oafish face peered in. He shined his light around inside, and his beam raked across orderly rows: sleeping chicken, sleeping chicken, teapot, sleeping chicken. Wait. *Teapot?* He panned the flashlight back. The pot now had a tea cozy on it—a tea cozy that looked very much like a chicken. Steam rose from its head. The chicken below made small clucking noises.

Mr. Tweedy's eyes narrowed. He *knew* something was going on. These chickens weren't as dumb as they looked.

Just then, Mrs. Tweedy's voice came wafting in from across the farm like a bad smell. "Mr. Tweedy!"

Aaaaak! It was *her*! Mr. Tweedy jumped in terror, and the door slammed on his head. Then he straightened up and tried to get a grip on himself. "It's all in your head, it's all in your head," he chanted to himself.

As the chickens held their breath, the roof to the hut closed, and Mr. Tweedy was gone.

A lantern was lit. Ginger paced up and down in front of the group. "We can't go on like this," she said. "Think, everyone. What haven't we tried yet?"

The chickens collectively tried to think. But this was difficult. Even though they were smart chickens, they were still chickens.

"We haven't tried *not* trying to escape," offered Bunty. She was completely serious.

"Ooh, that might work!" said Babs.

There were murmurs of agreement from the group:

"That's a very good idea...."

"Me bum is sore from that last one...."

Ginger could not believe what she was hearing. "What are you all saying then, that we should just give up?" she demanded. She pointed to an empty nest nearby. "What about Edwina? How many more empty nests will it take?"

"Perhaps," said Bunty, "it wouldn't *be* empty if she'd spent more time layin' and less time escapin'." Bunty turned to address the other hens. "Look," she said, "we've always been egg layers, our mothers were egg layers. And if it was good enough for them, by gum, it should be good enough for us."

"So laying eggs all your life and then getting plucked, stuffed, and roasted is good enough for you, is it?" said Ginger.

"It's a living," said Babs naively. There were more nods and murmurs of agreement from the others.

Ginger was so exasperated she could hardly speak. It's a *living*? she thought. Giving up your life to be someone's dinner is a *living*?

"You know what the problem is?" she said at last. "The fences aren't just round the farm. They're up here," she told him, pointing at her skull, "in your heads. There's a better place out there—somewhere beyond that hill." Her voice rose along with her emotion, as she painted the picture she had held in her mind for so long. "And, and it has wide open spaces and lots of trees. And *grass*. Can you imagine that? Cool green grass!" By this time, Ginger was lost in her vision.

"Who feeds us?" interrupted Ducky.

"We feed ourselves," Ginger tried.

"Where's the farm?" asked Agnes. None of them had ever lived in a place that wasn't a farm. They simply could imagine what life could be like in such a place.

"There is no farm."

"Then where does the farmer live?" Babs wanted to know.

"There is no farmer, Babs," Ginger explained as patiently as she could.

Babs was having difficulty. "Is he on holiday?"

"He isn't anywhere."

"Then who collects the eggs?" Ducky challenged.

Ginger tried again to get through. "There's no morning egg count, no dogs, no farmers, and no fences!" she said passionately.

Bunty stepped up to the front. "I've never heard such a fantastic—load of *tripe*." She turned to Ginger. "Face the facts, ducks—the chances of us getting out of here are a million to one."

The chickens awaited Ginger's response as she squared off with Bunty. "Then there's still a chance," she said in a steady voice.

Ginger stared at them all for a moment, and then walked out of the hut. It was just no use. What was wrong with them? There was freedom out there, somewhere! She could almost taste it! She had a dream, she had a vision.

Why couldn't they see it too?

Once outside, she paced up and down, her head buried in her hands. "Oh no, oh no, oh no," she moaned to herself, "what am I doing? Oh, who are you trying to fool?" she said to herself. "You can't lead this bunch of—"

She walked over to the fence, grabbed it, looked up, and heaved a big sigh. "Heaven, help us," she entreated.

There was an immediate flash of lightning, then a thunderclap. Ginger turned around just in time to see a figure flying toward her. It was screaming.

"*Freeeedommmm!*" shrieked the figure.

Ginger's eyes widened. Was this . . . a *rooster*?

Yes, it was. At least, she thought so. He was still in motion, little more than a screeching brown-and-green streak above her in the air. He sailed over her head, giving her a little salute as he went. He seemed to be wearing some sort of cape, which looked to have a pattern of stars and stripes on it.

Then—*thwang!* He slammed into the weathervane, which looked a bit like him but much more composed. He spun around the weathervane a few times, got flung back the other way, and then—*sproinggg!*—hit the power lines, which rocketed him back in the opposite direction. Finally he plummeted headfirst into the feeders, his cape in tatters.

The whole time he was bouncing back and forth, he'd been yelling. "*Ahhhhhhhh!*" he went.

A light went on inside the Tweedys' farmhouse.

Meanwhile, the other chickens hurried out of Hut 17, just in time to see the rooster flip out of the feeder and land on his feet in front of Ginger. He dusted himself off a bit. "Thank you, ladies and gentlemen, you've been a wonderful audience!" he said with as much bravado as he could muster.

He held the pose for a moment, and then, *Slam!* The upended feeder crashed down on top of him, sending billows of dust into the air. The chickens rushed over to it.

As the dust settled, something fell from the sky and landed right in Ginger's hands. It was a torn poster. Her eyes widened as she looked at it. What was pictured on it could be the means of their salvation. And it all had to do with this rooster.

"*That's it!*" she cried.

Ginger
Makes a Deal

Across the yard, the front door to the farm opened, and out came Mr. Tweedy with his flashlight. He headed toward the huts to investigate. There was no time to lose.

Ginger put one of the rooster's wings over her shoulder. "Get him inside," she said to the others. "Quickly."

Moving with haste, the chickens carried the newcomer inside Hut 17. They pulled the curtains closed just as Mr. Tweedy's light swept past.

When he was gone, Ginger held up the poster for all the other chickens to see.

On it was a brightly colored picture of the rooster, flying through the air. Above the picture was a caption that read, "Rocky the Flying Rooster!"

"*This*," said Ginger, "is our way out of here."

"We'll make posters?" asked Babs.

"What's *on* the poster, Babs, what's *on* the poster! We'll *fly* out."

There were hushed murmurs from the other chickens, as they tried to figure out what on earth Ginger could be talking about.

"He must be very important to have his picture taken," said Babs. "What do you suppose he does?"

Bunty chipped in. "Isn't it obvious? He's a professional flying rooster. He flies from farm to farm giving demonstrations."

"Do you suppose?" Babs mused.

"Oh, absolutely," replied Bunty.

Ginger sighed. Once again, there would be some patient explaining to do.

Rocky the Flying Rooster stirred and moaned.

"He's waking up!" cried Ducky.

Rocky moaned some more and groggily opened his eyes a bit. "Mmmm...dark...no...not in there, not in there... gotta get...gotta get..." he mumbled deliriously.

His eyes opened more and he took in the blurry sight of several chickens staring back at him. "Aaaahhhh!" he screamed. He leaped to his feet and backed toward the wall. "Who are y— Where am I?...What's going—*Ouch!*" He clutched his arm and then noticed the bandage on it. "What happened to my wing?" he cried.

This threw most of the chickens into a state of new confusion.

Ginger stepped in to explain. "You took a rather nasty fall," she told Rocky.

"And," added Mac in her fast, thick Scottish accent, "sprained the anterior tendon connecting your radius to your humerus."

"Was that English?" Rocky asked Ginger.

"She said you sprained your wing," Ginger translated. "She fixed it."

"And I made the bandage!" Babs said proudly, holding up her knitting needles.

"I-I-I carried you in!" Bunty chipped in.

Now all the other chickens crowded in on him, anxious to share the credit.

"I fluffed the hay!"

"I rubbed your feet!"

"I sang you to sleep!"

Fowler had now entered the hut. He stood near the door, scowling at the newcomer. He did not like what he was seeing, not at all.

Rocky was unaware of this negative element in the scene, though. All he saw was the gaggle of chickens who were vying for his approval. He chuckled, enjoying the attention. "Whoa, whoa, whoa, whoa—whoa, girls. Let's back up and start from the top. Where am I?"

"You're right, how rude of us," said Ginger. "We're just very exci—" she stopped to collect herself. "This is a chicken farm."

"And we're the chickens," added Babs, always helpful.

"Uh-huh, with you so far," Rocky said. "Chicken farm, chickens..."

Fowler now broke through the crowd and squared off beak to beak with Rocky. "I don't like the look of this one," the old rooster told the others. "His eyes are too close together."

Ginger tried to stop him from insulting their great new hope. "Fowler, please..."

"And he's a *Yank*," Fowler harrumphed.

"Easy, pops," said Rocky. "Cockfighting is illegal where I come from."

"And where is that exactly?" Bunty wanted to know.

"Just a little place I call the land of the free and the home of the brave." Rocky smirked.

"Scotland!" cried Mac joyfully.

Rocky looked at her in incomprehension. "No—America," he said.

The chickens were very impressed. "Oooh, America," they said. "How exciting."

Disgusted, Fowler flung Rocky's arm off his own. "Poppycock!" he said, and turned to leave, muttering. "Pushy Americans, always showing up late for every war. Overpaid, oversexed—and over here!" And with that, he stormed out.

Rocky was not much disturbed. "Hey, what's eating Grandpa?" he asked.

"Don't mind him, Mr. . . . Mr. . . . ?" said Ginger.

"The name's Rocky. Rocky the Rhode Island Red. Rhodes for short."

"Rocky Rhodes?" said Agnes.

Rocky grinned. "Catchy, ain't it?"

The chickens all nodded eagerly.

Ginger held up the poster. "Mr. Rhodes, is this you?" she asked him.

Rocky recoiled from the picture. "Who wants to know?" he asked suspiciously.

"A group of rather desperate chickens," Ginger explained. "You see, if it *is* you, then you just might be the answer to our prayers." She was already pinning all her hopes on him, so eager for his help that she left her usual no-nonsense self behind.

Rocky looked around at all the chickens smiling back at him, batting their eyes. This was not such a bad situation, not bad at all. He pointed to the poster and smiled a big charming all-American smile at Ginger. "Well, then call me a miracle, doll face—'cause that's me!"

At that, the chickens broke into spontaneous applause.

"And what brings you to England, Mr. Rhodes?" Beatrice inquired when the clapping had died down.

"Why, all the beautiful English chicks, of course," said Rocky. He smiled again, and the chickens swooned.

"Oh, you!" said the smitten Bunty. "Give over!" She smacked Rocky on the back, so hard he nearly lost his breath.

Now all the hens crowded around him. "Tell us more about America, Mr. Rhodes," they said. "How did you get here? What's it like?"

Rocky moved casually among the hens. He was really working the coop now, playing up the easy American fly-boy charm for all it was worth. "See, I'm a traveler by nature," he said. "I did that whole 'barnyard thing' for a while but couldn't really get into it." He paused to give one of the chickens a particularly dazzling smile. "Hi, how are ya?" he said, with a wink and a nudge. Then he went back into his routine. "Nope. The open road—that's more my style. Just give me a pack on my back, and point me where the wind blows."

The chickens were completely awestruck. "In fact," Rocky continued, "you know what they call me back home? You're gonna love this." He paused for effect. "The Lone Free Ranger."

"Ooooh," said all the chickens.

Even Rocky was a bit thrown by the awe this boasting inspired. "Yeah," he said modestly, "isn't that great? I just love it."

Ginger was electrified. "Did you hear that, everyone? A free chicken. I *knew* it was possible."

"Oh, it's possible, all right," said Rocky.

"And I knew the answer would come," Ginger went on, fully relishing her vindication.

"Amen!" said Rocky.

"We're all going to fly over that fence," said Ginger, "because Mr. Rhodes is going to show us how!"

"That's rrr—*what?!* Did you say *fly?*"

"You can teach us," Ginger said, beaming.

Rocky looked around. The chickens were nodding eagerly. "Um... No, I can't, my flying days are over," he vamped.

The chickens crowded around him, pleading for his help, as he hastily gathered his things.

But Rocky was cocking an ear to the door. "You hear that?" he said.

The chickens leaned forward, trying to hear.

"Shh, listen. Hear it?" Rocky continued. He paused for effect. "That's the open road calling my name, and I was born to answer that call. Bye." He dashed out the door.

Babs was still trying to listen through door. "He must have very good hearing," she said.

The other chickens mumbled nervously, and Ginger silenced them with a raised hand. "Wait here," she told them.

Outside, Rocky was strutting toward the fence. "Okay, okay," he muttered to himself. "Where's the exit? Ah, this way..."

Ginger marched up from behind him. "Mr. Rhodes," she said, "perhaps I didn't explain our situation properly." She paused to catch her breath. "We lay eggs, day in and day out, and when we can't lay anymore"—she looked him

straight in the eye, making sure she had his full attention—
"they kill us," she concluded.

"Hey, it's a cruel world, doll face," said Rocky flippantly.
"Might as well get used to it."

He kept right on walking, but Ginger hadn't given up.
She had been on the farm for too long and had seen too
much to give up that easily.

She followed him until she was able to get in front of
him and block his path. "Which part of 'they kill us' do you
not understand?" she demanded.

"Hey, I got my own set of problems to worry about.
Besides, this birdcage can't be that hard to bust out of. In
fact, watch me."

"It's not so hard to get one chicken out of here, or even
two, but this is about all of us," said Ginger.

Rocky stopped in his tracks and spun around, stunned.
"*All* of you?"

"That's what I've been trying to tell you."

"Wait a minute, let me get this straight. You want to
get every chicken in this place out of here—*at the same
time?*"

"Who else would I be doing it for?"

Rocky stared at her as her words sank in. "You're certi-
fiable!" he spluttered. "You can't pull off a stunt like that—
it's suicide!"

"Where there's a will, there's a way."

"Couldn't agree more," said Rocky. "And I *will* be leaving—*that* way." He walked toward the fence.

Ginger could see her last hope walking away. "But, Mr. Rhodes . . . please . . ." she begged.

This pitiful scene was interrupted at that moment by the arrival of a large van, which drove by the farm and then pulled into the driveway. On its side was a logo that showed a lion jumping through a ring of fire, and two elephants rearing up on their hind legs. The words on the van read, Colonel Daniel Spoon's Travelling Circus.

Rocky froze for a second, and then dove behind a hut. But Ginger stayed in the open. She looked at the van, and then she looked at Rocky's face, peeking out from the corner. Suddenly he didn't look so sure of himself anymore. Ginger was putting two and two together.

"So that's it," she said. "You're from the circus."

Rocky leaped out, grabbed her, and yanked her into the shadows. "*Shhh!*" he whispered.

The van stopped in the farmyard driveway as Rocky kept a nervous eye on it. Out came the circus man. Mr. and Mrs. Tweedy came out of the house to greet him.

"You're on the run, aren't you?" Ginger asked Rocky.

"You wanna keep it down?" Rocky whispered. "I'm trying to lay low here."

"I should turn you in right now!" said Ginger indignantly.

"You wouldn't," whispered Rocky. Then, on second thought, he added, "Would you?"

"Give me one reason why I shouldn't."

"Because I'm cute?"

"BRAAAAK!" Ginger squawked loudly. So much for the power of cute. *You don't help me, I don't help you*, Ginger thought to herself.

The Tweedys and the circus man turned toward the noise.

"Hey, hey, hey, hey," Rocky whispered urgently, keeping one eye on the man. "What kinda crazy chick are you? Do you know what'll happen if he finds me?"

"It's a cruel world," Ginger said with a shrug, echoing Rocky's words.

"I just decided—I don't like you," Rocky said to her.

"I just decided—I don't care," she countered. "Unfortunately, I need you. Now, show us how to fly."

Rocky protested. "With this wing?"

"*Teach* us, then."

"No!"

"BRAAAK!!" squawked Ginger, a little louder this time.

Rocky reached out and held her beak shut. "Now you listen here, sister," he said through gritted teeth. "I'm not going back to that life. I'm a Lone Free Ranger—emphasis on *free*."

Ginger was firm. "And that's what we want—freedom."

The Tweedys and the circus man were now moving toward the chicken compound, holding a flashlight. "Fancy that," said Ginger with some relish. "They're coming this way."

Rocky was now completely panicked. "Oh no! They're on to me! Oh m'gosh!"

"Teach us how to fly and we'll hide you," Ginger said quickly.

"And if I don't...?"

Ginger took a big breath, so she could gather up a nice loud squawk. "Braa..." she began, warming up, and then took another breath to squawk again.

Rocky once again grabbed her beak. "Was your father by any chance a vulture?" he said sourly.

Ginger pushed his hand away. "Do we have a deal?"

She extended a wing for Rocky to shake. He hesitated, checking over his shoulder: Could he get out of this? The circus man was getting closer all the time; there really was no choice.

Rocky shook on it, and Ginger immediately yanked him deeper into the shadows.

The Tweedys and the circus man were still heading straight for them, though.

"Time to make good on that deal, doll f—" Rocky began, but Ginger grabbed *his* beak before he could finish.

"The name," she said in a slow and deadly voice, "is Ginger!"

They were now backed up to Hut 17. Ginger knocked on the wall behind her. A slat fell open, and Rocky and Ginger were quickly pulled inside by many outstretched chicken wings. The door fell closed just as Mrs. Tweedy rounded the corner with the flashlight.

Everything was now completely quiet. The roof of the hut opened, and Mrs. Tweedy peered inside. Nothing looked out of the ordinary. The roof closed. Her footsteps moved off.

Inside the hut, Ginger bent down and opened a small hatch door in the floor. "Comfortable?" she asked.

There was Rocky, crammed into a tiny space. "Not really," he replied.

Ginger produced a shoehorn. "Maybe this will help," she said, shoving it under Rocky.

"Ooomph!" said Rocky as she pried him out. He tried his parts to see if they still worked. "Nice hideout. I had more room in my egg."

"We've held up our end of the deal," said the unsympathetic Ginger. "Tomorrow you'll hold up yours."

"What deal?"

Ginger was incensed. He was still trying to weasel out of it! "The flying!" she reminded him.

"Right, right, right. Don't worry. I'll teach you everything I know." He looked around the hut. "Now," he said, "which bunk is mine?"

All the hens eagerly leaned out of their bunks and waved fetchingly.

But Ginger had other ideas, and bedtime found Rocky and Fowler awkwardly huddled together in one bunk.

"Absolutely outrageous!" groused Fowler, giving Rocky

a shove. "Asking a senior officer to share his quarters—and with a noncommissioned Yank no less! Why, back in my day—"

"Hey!" interrupted Rocky, shoving back. "You weren't exactly my first choice either. And scoot over. Your wing is on my side of the bunk."

"*Your* side of the bunk? The whole bunk is my side of the bunk!" Fowler pointed out.

"What's that smell?" Rocky shot back. "Is that your breath?"

"Absolutely outrageous!" Fowler sputtered.

There was more pushing, more shoving, more battling for inches of space, more grumbling, more insulting.

And so it went, until night turned to day.

Flying Lessons

It was time to begin. Rocky paced back and forth before the hens, looking haggard. He'd had a rough night, without much sleep. But Ginger was not going to let him out of his first lesson, so there was nothing to do but make the best of it.

"So," he began, "you wanna fly, huh?" He kept pacing, vamping as he tried to figure out what to say in view of the fact that he knew nothing about the subject. "Well, it ain't gonna be easy. And it ain't gonna happen overnight, either." Aha. Finally, an idea. "Flying," he said authoritatively, "takes three things. Hard work. Perseverance. And ... hard work," he said, his big idea petering out.

Fowler was watching all this from the doorway. "You said hard work twice!" he heckled.

Rocky didn't miss a beat. "That's because it takes twice as much work as perseverance," he responded.

"Codswallop!" said Fowler. "Cocky Yanks, think they know it all, always have a snappy answer, why back in my day..." And off he walked, grumbling to himself.

Rocky was still going. "And most importantly," he continued, "we have to work as a team—which means you do *everything I tell you*." He settled in and leaned against a hut, getting comfortable. "Right," he said. "Let's rock 'n' roll."

And so, the chickens tried to rock 'n' roll. Rocky started them on a strict exercise regime: simple moves at first, like deep knee bends and arm raises. Rocky tried to demonstrate, but when he lifted his wing, he winced, much to Ginger's consternation.

"Keep going," said Rocky, gritting his teeth through the pain.

The chickens lay on their backs, pedaling their feet in midair. They did toe-touches as Rocky moved behind them, admiring the view, and Ginger scowled.

Next came the squat-thrusts. Bending at the knees, they thrust their wings out to the side—all except for Babs, who continued to knit, ducking each squat to avoid getting smacked by the chickens beside her.

Push-ups next. Bunty did them one-handed as the rest of the chickens strained and puffed.

Rocky was now reclining off to the side, perched on some soft, comfortable grain sacks. An adoring chicken fanned him with a feather duster.

"One-two-three," he counted, "keep it *up*, two-three..."

Just outside the fence, Mr. Tweedy was pushing his egg cart along. He casually looked to his left, glancing into the yard as he normally did. Dum-de-dum-de-dum, just going along with the egg cart.

And then, it registered. What on earth had he just seen? Could that possibly have been a row of chickens doing push-ups? Mr. Tweedy shook his head, hard, and then did a huge double-take. There they were, all right. Doing push-ups.

Mrs. Tweedy, as it happened, was right behind him. This was exciting! Now was his big chance to show her that he wasn't crazy! Wordlessly, he pointed toward the yard.

She looked. The chickens were now pecking innocently at the dirt.

Mrs. Tweedy gave Mr. Tweedy a withering look as he scratched his head in confusion.

Then it was back to work for the chickens, as soon as they were sure the Tweedys had gone. They stood in formation, rhythmically flapping their wings to Rocky's commands.

"And *right*-two-three and *left*-two-three. And right-two-three ... and left, left, left. Ooh! Down! Down!"

The chickens did their best to comply, stepping right, stepping left, left, left, then crouching down, and down some more, until they were scrunched as far as possible into the ground.

Ginger watched all this in confusion. These were some very strange exercises. How was this like flying?

"Stop right there! Ooh, yeah. Make little circles!" Rocky said now.

The chickens stopped right there, and then spun around in circles.

"Oh, faster!" said Rocky.

The chickens spun faster. They had absolutely no idea that Rocky was sitting in a pail of hot water, his own personal rooster-sized hot tub. His eyes were closed. One chicken was pumping a bicycle pump in order to create bubbles, while another massaged his shoulder.

"Oooh, faster," said Rocky, still talking to the massager.

The poor exercising chickens spun faster still.

Ginger had had enough. She stomped over to Rocky.

Rocky opened one eye and saw her standing in front of him. "There a problem, doll face?" he asked cheerfully.

"*Ginger*," said Ginger, her beak clenched. She was getting really, really sick of being called "doll face."

Abruptly, she turned to the two hens who were pampering Rocky. "Back in line, you two," she ordered.

One chicken stopped massaging and got back in line.

The other chicken stopped blowing bubbles and then passed out.

"Funny," said Rocky grumpily to Ginger, "I don't remember saying 'stop the massage.'"

Ginger ignored that comment. "I thought you were going to teach us how to fly," she said sharply.

"That's what I'm doing."

"Isn't there usually some *flapping* involved?"

"Hey, do I tell you how to lay eggs?" Rocky leaned back, wings behind his head. "Relax, we're making progress."

"Really? I can't help thinking we're going round in circles."

Rocky glanced over and noticed, to his surprise, that the chickens were indeed spinning in circles. "Ummm, yeah," he said, trying to look nonchalant, "I think they're ready to fly now."

The chickens fell down.

"Good," said Ginger sarcastically. "Because they certainly can't walk anymore."

It was time for Rocky to save face. He stood up and called out to the chickens. "Up and at 'em, gals. Let's flap!"

And so, the flapping phase began.

First there was the ramp. This was a wooden plank, its end propped up high in the air. One by one, the chickens took a running start up the makeshift incline, flapping madly as they ascended to the top. Off the end they plummeted, as Rocky gave them a cheerful thumbs-up. This was all going just fine, in his view. Anything to get Ginger off his back.

Along came Nick and Fetcher, the busy businessrats, looking for Ginger. "Right, Fetcher," said Nick. "Let's see if ol' Attila the Hen has come to her senses."

Meanwhile, the chickens continued to screech as they plunged, one after the other, off the end of the ramp. One of them landed almost at the rats' feet, and then more and more followed, falling all around them.

"It's raining hen!" snickered Fetcher.

"Hallelujah!" Nick sang out.

Babs moved amid the commotion, still knitting.

"What's this caper, luv?" Nick asked her.

"We're flying," she replied serenely as Bunty landed at their feet with a resounding thud.

"Obviously," said Nick.

Babs moved off, and the rats watched some more.

"They're gonna kill themselves," Fetcher remarked to Nick. He considered this possibility. "Wanna watch?"

Nick thought about it for a moment. "Yeah, all right," he said, shrugging.

From another part of the yard, Rocky and Ginger were also watching the rain of chickens. Rocky bravely gave Ginger the thumbs-up. Ginger wasn't buying it.

The next brilliantly conceived exercise involved hot water bottles. The chickens would bounce over the fence, using the hot water bottles as launching pads. By this time, Nick and Fetcher had set up makeshift bleachers, so they could be more comfortable as they heckled the chickens.

"It's poultry in motion!" cackled Nick. A chicken tumbled toward them, landing in front of the bleachers. "Careful of those eggs," he admonished her. After all, they were soon to be his eggs.

Then there was a new flapping exercise. Bunty ran across the yard, carrying a chicken overhead. But instead of flapping, the chicken was doing the breaststroke. She was not getting any height with this method, but it looked very nice.

"Look! Sunny-side up," Nick commented.

"No. Over easy," Fetcher opined. Ginger shot them a look as they cackled and slapped each other on the back.

The flying lessons continued. Rocky's next big idea was the Roof Run. This meant that the chickens ran along the ridge of a rooftop and flapped wildly as they went over the edge. They fell like lead weights.

"Go, go, go, go, go, go . . . GO!" Rocky yelled from the ground.

"Oi! Go-go chicks!" Nick heckled.

Ginger was trying hard to ignore them. She climbed up to the rooftop, took a running start, flapped, and fell a few inches, landing on something soft and—moving? She looked down to find that it was a pile of chickens. She sighed.

"Birds of a feather *flop* together!" cackled Fetcher.

At last, after gathering their strength again, the chickens pulled themselves out of the pile and headed back toward their huts, clutching their backs and moaning.

"Great work, ladies," said Rocky. "Great work. The pain you're feeling is good. Pain is your friend." He began working the crowd in the way he knew so well. "Just keep the faith, uh ... what's your name there? Agnes, Agnes. You're doin' great. And, Ducky, I think you flew four feet today."

The rats were still off to the side in their bleachers. "Right!" called Nick. "Four feet! From the roof to the ground!" More cackling from the rats.

"All part of the process, ladies," said Rocky nonchalantly. "Nothing to worry about."

Chapter 6

Turn Your Chicken Farm into a Gold Mine

Suddenly, a loud sound thundered through the farm. It was some sort of rumbling, very deep, very loud. So loud, it set the surface of a nearby puddle quivering.

"Whoa, that doesn't sound good," said Rocky.

The chickens froze. They looked around, tense and confused. Now the ground was shaking. Rocky, not so nonchalant anymore, gulped hard. "Okay, the ground's shaking. Are we worried, are we worried . . . ?"

A pair of headlights washed over them as the source of the rumbling presented itself. It was an enormous truck, and it was pulling slowly and deliberately into the farm's driveway.

"The circus!" gasped Rocky. He grabbed Ginger. "Hide me! *Hide me!*" he pleaded.

Ginger grabbed Rocky and dragged him toward Fowler's hut.

Inside, Fowler was busy regarding himself in the mirror, examining his RAF medal. "One isn't awarded a medal like this for flapping about like a lunatic, what," he was grumbling to himself.

In burst Ginger, with Rocky in tow. She looked around the room for a suitable place to stuff Rocky.

"Now, see here. This is an officer's quarters," Fowler protested.

Ginger spotted an open bombshell in the corner, a relic from Fowler's war days.

"Quick. In here!" Ginger said, dragging Rocky toward it.

Fowler wasn't having any. "Get out of here immediately, sir!" he ordered.

"Ah, give it a rest, pops," Rocky returned.

Ginger slammed the hatch to the bombshell and sprinted out of Fowler's hut.

"I shall have you on a charge within the week!" Fowler shouted after her.

Ginger was already outside, though, doing some reconnaissance work. She made her way over to the barn, where the huge truck was now backing up. The words Poultry & Products were written on the side.

It wasn't the circus. What was it? Ginger was getting nervous.

In her office, Mrs. Tweedy peered over the top of her magazine, the one that said "Turn Your Chicken Farm into a Gold Mine" on the front. She smiled greedily as the truck edged toward the barn door.

When the truck had come to a stop, the Tweedys went outside to supervise the unloading operation. The workers lifted a huge crate off the back of the truck and loaded it into the barn.

In the middle of all this activity, Mr. Tweedy happened to glance over into the chicken yard. There were Ginger and Mac, peering intently through binoculars at the truck. The other chickens were gathered around them.

Mr. Tweedy's eyes widened as Ginger and Mac quickly hid the binoculars.

Chickens with binoculars? This was simply too much for Mr. Tweedy to handle. There was nothing for Mr. Tweedy to do but tell himself that he had imagined it, and try shake it off. "It's all in your head, it's all in your head," he chanted softly to himself.

Inside the barn, Mrs. Tweedy lost no time in wedging a tire iron into the crate and prying the front off.

"Oooh, what's all this then?" asked Mr. Tweedy, peering inside.

"This is our future, Mr. Tweedy," his wife informed him. "No more wastin' time with petty egg collection and minuscule profits."

"No more eggs?" said Mr. Tweedy. "But ... we've always been egg farmers. My father, and his father, and all their fathers, they was always—"

"Poor! Worthless! Nothings!" his wife interrupted curtly. "But all that's about to change." She caressed the crate lovingly. "This will take Tweedy's farm out of the dark ages and into full-scale automated production." She turned back to Mr. Tweedy with savage intensity. "Melisha Tweedy will be poor no longer," she spat at him. Then she shoved a manual into his chest and stomped out of the barn.

"I'll put it together then, shall I?" he asked, lost as ever.

His only answer was the loud slam of the barn door.

Mac and Ginger were still standing at the fence, watching. "This isn't good, Mac," said Ginger. "Whatever's in those boxes is for us—and I don't think it's softer hay."

"Aye, hen," Mac agreed. "And I hate to be the voice o' doom, but I've been calculatin' m' figures"—she checked her notepad—"and I just dunnea think we're built for flyin'."

"But I *saw* him!" cried Ginger defensively. "He flew in over that fence!"

"Aye, aye—I believe ya. But if we could see it for ourselves, that might answer some questions."

"You're right," Ginger said. "I'm sorry. We've been at this all week and we're getting nowhere. If Rocky's wing were better he could..."

She petered out, thinking. Then she sighed. It was all so difficult. "I'll have a word with him," she said.

Mac continued working on her figures as Ginger headed off to find Rocky.

Fowler was sitting on his bunk, polishing another medal, when Ginger stepped into his hut. She looked into the old bombshell where she'd stashed Rocky, but Rocky wasn't in it.

"Where is he?" she demanded of Fowler.

"They didn't give me this medal for being a Yank nanny!" he replied irritably.

"A simple 'I don't know' would suffice," she retorted just as irritably. Then she turned to leave.

"Beware of that one, young Ginger," Fowler warned. "That Yank is not to be trusted."

"That 'Yank' is our ticket out of here," she told him.

At that very moment, the "Yank" was sitting on a bunk in one of the chicken huts, having a swell time telling jokes.

". . . and the pig says to the horse, 'Hey, fella, why the long face?' AH HA HA HA!" roared Rocky, doubling over with laughter at his own wit. He was surrounded by adoring hens, who were also tittering and laughing.

Emboldened by his success, Rocky plucked a tail feather out of his rear and plopped it into his drink. "Look! Cocktail!" he said.

Bunty, who was standing beside him, gave him a huge whack on the back, causing him to spray his drink everywhere. "Give over!" she said.

The crowd parted to dodge Rocky's drink-shower, and there stood Ginger, hands on hips. Her foot was tapping.

Rocky instantly snapped into a more serious pose, trying to cover for himself. "So, um . . . anyway," he mumbled to the group, "remember those *flying tips* tomorrow—they're very important. And keep thinking those flighty thoughts."

The chickens dispersed, but Ginger kept staring Rocky down.

In the face of Ginger's wrath, Rocky tried to act cool. "They're swell chicks, they really are," he said. "Look at what Babs made me." He held up an oddly shaped knitted item. "A beak warmer," he explained. "Isn't that the cutest? And that Bunty," he continued, rubbing his shoulder. "Whoa. She really packs a pun—" He ground to a halt in midsentence, unable to stand Ginger's glare anymore. She had not removed her hands from her hips. "Is there problem here?" he said.

"Have we flown over that fence?" she asked him.

"Not quite."

"Then there's a problem," said Ginger.

"Good things come to those who wait, doll face," said Rocky, heading for the door with all due haste.

Ginger stomped her foot. "Ginger!" she called after him.

Rocky was now strutting across the compound, hoping he'd put an end to the conversation. But Ginger was not done with him. She caught up with him very quickly.

"Okay—how long did it take you?" she asked him.

"To do what?"

"To learn how to fly!"

"Apples and oranges, baby doll," said Rocky with a wave of the hand. "I'm gifted, they're not. You can't compare the two, okay?" He turned and began to walk away from Ginger. "Look," he added, "the point is—these things take time."

"Which we are rapidly running out of. And we haven't even lifted off the ground! *Why?*"

At this moment they were joined by Mac. "Throost!" she exclaimed.

"What?" said Rocky and Ginger.

"I went o'er m'calculations, hen," Mac said to Ginger, "and figured the key element we're missing is throost."

"I didn't get a word of that," said Rocky.

"Throost!" Mac repeated. "Other birds like ducks and geese—when they take off, that's what they have. Throost."

"I swear she ain't usin' real words," muttered Rocky.

Ginger translated from the Scottish. "She said we need more thrust," she told Rocky.

"Oh, *thrust*," he said, still clueless of course. "Well . . . why didn't she . . . I mean . . . Of course we need thrust. Thrust and flying are like, like—like this." He put his feathers together, making a point. "That's flying, that's thrust."

Ginger grabbed Rocky by the wing—the hurt one. "Will you excuse us?" she said to Mac. Then she pulled Rocky aside.

"The wing, the wing, the wing!" Rocky protested.

Ginger spun him around. "If we don't see some results by tomorrow, the deal is off and you're on your own. No more hiding, the farmers will find you, and it's back to the circus, flyboy."

"You know," said Rocky meanly, "you're the first chick I ever met with the shell still on."

She continued to scowl at him.

Rocky tried a new tack, giving her a coy smile. "Sleep tight, angel face. The Rock's on the case." Then he gave her a wink before he walked away.

Ginger stomped her foot. "Ginger!" she yelled.

Throost

I t was early morning in Hut 17. Ginger stood before the mirror, practicing her flapping.

Through the window, a familiar voice wafted in on the breeze. It was Nick, the avaricious rat.

"Oh it was a beaut, guvnah," he was saying to someone. "A fine piece of work if I do say so m'self."

"I say so, too," Fetcher's voice chimed in.

"Well, c'mon, guys. Don't keep me in suspense," said a third voice. "Gimme the details."

Ginger realized with some surprise that the third voice was Rocky's. He was standing outside the hut with Nick and Fetcher, laughing it up.

"We slipped into the farmer's room, all quiet like," Nick said.

"Like a fish," added Fetcher.

"And we . . . like a fish?" said Nick, his train of thought

broken. "What do you mean like a fi—." He shook it off. "Ya stupid Norbert . . . Anyway, guv. Here it is. El merchandiso."

"That's Spanish," chirped Fetcher, always helpful.

The three of them were interrupted by a voice behind them. "What are these two extortionists doing here?" it demanded.

They spun around to see Ginger, who had come outside to investigate.

"Whoa. Back in the knife drawer, Miss Sharp," said Rocky.

"She don't appreciate talent like you do, sir," said Fetcher.

"Guys," said Rocky, "you are without a doubt the sneakiest, most light-fingered, thieving parasites I've ever met."

"You're too kind," said Nick modestly.

"I've gone bright red," said Fetcher, not that anyone could see this.

"So, uh, how 'bout them eggs?" Nick asked Rocky.

Ginger exploded. "Eggs?! Don't tell me you promised them—"

"Afraid I did," said Rocky breezily. "Promised them *every egg I lay this month*." He winked at Ginger and walked away. Ginger followed on his heels.

"And when can we expect the first installment, sir?" Nick called after him.

Dwindling profits at Tweedy's Farm.

Ginger attempts to tunnel to freedom.

GINGER

"FREEDOM!!"

"This is our way out of here."

ROCKY

"Show us how to fly."

"Great work, ladies. Great work."

Nick and Fetcher supply "el merchandiso."

"Go with it, baby!"

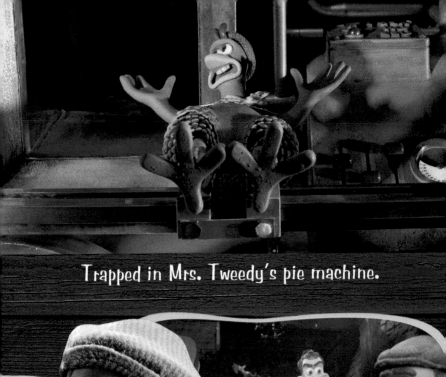

Trapped in Mrs. Tweedy's pie machine.

"Turn it off! TURN IT OFF!"

MR. TWEEDY

Rocky and Ginger celebrate
their narrow escape.

Mac sketches out plans for the "crate."

MRS. TWEEDY

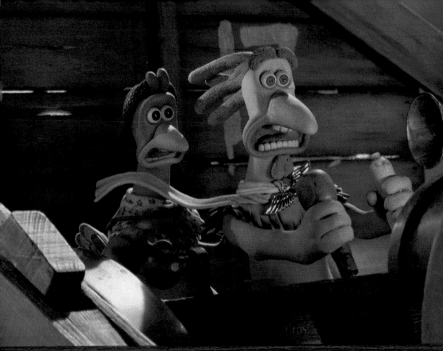

"Wing Commander T. I. Fowler, reporting for duty."

Free at last!

"Brewing one up as we speak, guys!" Rocky called back to him. "I'll keep you posted!"

When they were a little distance away, Ginger stepped in front of him. "You *lied* to them," she said furiously.

"No, I didn't."

"Yes, you did."

"No, I didn't."

"*Yes—you did,*" Ginger shouted.

Rocky was unfazed. "I didn't lie, doll face. I just omitted certain truths. They'll get exactly what I promised."

"Which is nothing."

"Which is what I'll give them."

"And what will you give us?" Ginger asked.

Rocky stuck his wings into imaginary suspenders and spoke in a Scottish accent. "*Throost,*" he said.

Later that morning, everything was ready.

Wearing an aviator's helmet and goggles that Babs had knitted for the occasion, Bunty lay on her belly on a bunk between two huts in the chicken yard. The bunk had been modified, and it now sat on wheels. Looped around back of the bunk was a pair of Mr. Tweedy's suspenders. What they had made was basically a large slingshot, with the bunk as the rock.

S-T-R-E-T-C-H...

The chickens pulled back on the bunk, stretching the

suspenders as far as they could.

Nick and Fetcher were sitting in their "bleachers," watching. "Hurry! The *tension's* killing me!" Nick cackled.

"Release!" Rocky ordered the chickens.

They let go.

Bunty rocketed forward across the yard. The length of rope that was attached to the back of the bunk uncoiled, and then—*thoing!*—went taut.

The bunk stopped short, shooting Bunty forward off it.

"*Flap!*" urged Ginger.

Bunty flapped and flapped, still shooting along.

"Poultry in motion," cracked Nick as she whizzed past him.

She kept flapping furiously, and then—*bloop!*—slammed into the chain-link fence.

"Minister of *de-fence*!" howled Fetcher.

Their howls of laughter turned into screams as Bunty bounced off the fence and hurtled back toward them. She slammed into them, sending them tumbling.

"Ooomph!" they went, and now it was the chickens' turn to laugh.

Suddenly, they all froze: *the bell!*

Ginger looked toward it, worried.

Meanwhile, Babs was panicking. "Roll call!" she gasped.

"Hide me!" Rocky pleaded with Ginger. But Ginger was only concerned with Babs.

"I haven't laid any eggs," Babs dithered. "Three days and not a one! Oh no . . ."

"Why didn't you tell us, Babs!" said Ginger.

"Hide me!" Rocky repeated annoyingly.

Babs wrung her wings. "We've been so busy . . . with the flying . . . and the . . ."

"They're coming!" cried Agnes.

"*Hide me!*" Rocky yelled again.

"*HIDE YOURSELF!*" Ginger yelled back.

The chickens scurried to get into line. Rocky frantically searched for a place to hide, finally diving into one of the feeders.

And then, the Tweedys were upon them.

Mrs. Tweedy marched up to the line, as she always did, while Mr. Tweedy peeled off to collect the eggs.

The farmer's wife paced up and down before the assembled group. She was just staring and smiling.

Babs quivered in her spot.

Mr. Tweedy handed her the clipboard. She eyed it. Babs gulped.

Then Mrs. Tweedy leaned down, as she had before. Only this time, she had—*a cloth measuring tape?*

She wrapped it around Babs's hips. When she'd gotten the measurement, she half-smiled.

Ginger was very worried. This was a first. This had never happened before. What did it all mean?

Mrs. Tweedy checked the measurement and turned to Mr. Tweedy. "Double their food rations," she snapped. "I want them all as fat as this one."

Then she turned on her heel and left, Mr. Tweedy following her.

Babs collapsed into Bunty's arms. "My life flashed before my eyes," she blithered. "It was really boring."

Lunchtime came. At the feeders, Mr. Tweedy ripped open a seed bag and poured in huge amounts of food.

Delighted and mystified, the chickens rushed the feeders and started pecking away like mad.

Meanwhile, Ginger was off to the side, thinking. At last she put two and two together. She hurried over to her friends.

"Wait . . . don't . . . STOP!" she screamed. She grabbed the feeder and turned it over, spilling all the seed onto the ground. Confused, the chickens stopped eating, some with their mouths full of seed.

"Can't you see what's going on here?" yelled Ginger. The chickens shook their heads.

"Listen," Ginger continued. She began listing things on her fingers. "Boxes arrive in the barn, Babs stops laying but they don't take her to the chop, and now they're giving us extra food! Don't you see what's happening? They're fattening us up. *They're going to kill us all!*"

The chickens gasped. Then they started murmuring among themselves:

"What is she saying?"

"Did she say kill?"

Rocky spat out his mouthful of seed at this. "Whoa, whoa, heavy alert," he said to the chickens. "She didn't mean it, gals. Keep eating, save some for me."

Grabbing Ginger, he pulled her away from the group. She sputtered indignantly. "What are you do—Let go of me!" she demanded.

He pulled her around the corner of the hut, where they couldn't be seen. "Listen," he told her, "I've met some hard-boiled eggs in my day, but I'd say you're about twenty minutes."

"What's that supposed to mean?" asked Ginger.

"It means you gotta lighten up! See, over in America, we have this rule: If you wanna motivate someone, don't . . . mention . . . death!"

Ginger was not moved by this wisdom. "Well, over here," she replied, "the rule is, always . . . tell . . . the truth."

"And, hey—that's been workin' like a charm, hasn't it? Here's some free advice. You want 'em to perform, tell 'em what they wanna hear."

"You mean, lie."

"Here we go again," said Rocky, throwing his hands up. He pointed an accusing feather at her. "You know what your problem is? You're *difficult*."

He walked away, but she followed him and cut him off. "Why?" she asked him. "Because I'm honest? I care about what happens to them, something I wouldn't expect a 'lone free ranger' to know anything about."

"Hey, if this is the way you show it," he said, "I hope you never *care* about me!"

"I can assure you, I never will!"

"Good!"

"Fine!"

That was it. The conversation was over. Ginger went one way, and Rocky went the other.

When Rocky rounded the corner of the hut, he was met with a dismal scene. There were all the hens, slumped over, heads bowed, looking depressed and lifeless.

As Rocky watched the hens, his face fell. He felt for them. Poor old girls.

He looked back at Ginger. Then an idea crept across his face, and he headed off in the opposite direction.

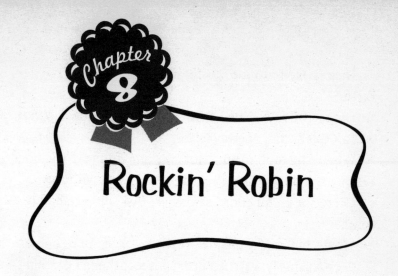

Rockin' Robin

That evening, Ginger sat on the roof of her hut, watching as the sun set behind her favorite hill. How many times had she stared at the geese flying toward that hill, watched as their strong wings propelled them effortlessly through the air? How many times had she wondered what it would be like to be free, like them?

Tonight her face was devoid of all expression. She was tired—tired of fighting, tired of thinking.

Then, behind her she heard some sort of a commotion. She turned to see what it was. There were Nick and Fetcher, carrying a transistor radio with great difficulty toward Hut 17.

"To me, to me, to me," Nick was directing. "Turn, mate . . . turn it!"

"'Ere, I've got all the weight here," Fetcher grunted.

Nick looked around. "Let's see, Hut 17, Hut 17—over there."

Ginger furrowed her brow and climbed down. What was all this about, anyway?

When she got inside Hut 17, she found Nick and Fetcher standing beside the radio. Rocky was with them.

"Here she is, guv'nor," said Nick. "Ask and ye shall receive."

"That's biblical," explained Fetcher.

Nick anxiously watched Rocky inspect the radio. "That's real craftsmanship, is what that is," he said. "Solid as a rock." Just to drive his point home, he gave the radio a whack. *Sproing!* Out shot a spring.

"It's supposed to do that," Fetcher said quickly.

"It's perfect, guys," said Rocky.

"And how's that egg coming?" asked Nick.

Rocky patted his stomach. "This is a *double* yolker," he said cheerfully.

Nick and Fetcher rubbed their hands together, practically salivating. They hurried out, a happy pair of rats.

When they were gone, Rocky knelt beside the radio. He began fiddling with the dials. In a moment, the crackle of static emitted from the box.

The chickens of Hut 17 recoiled, frightened.

Rocky twiddled the fine tuner, scanning through the stations.

Ginger entered the hut. "I don't see what this has to do with—"

"You will," Rocky told her.

As he moved the needle around the dial, various voices emanated from the red box. The hens were mesmerized.

Finally, he landed on some music.

"Perfect," said Rocky. He began to bounce to the beat, shaking his hips. "We've been workin' too hard," he announced. "Time to kick back a bit, shake those tail feathers, loosen it up—like this!" He now went into a little jig.

The hens whispered to one another. Bunty crossed her arms, scoffing. "Look at 'im. Nellypodging around like a . . ."

She looked down. Her foot was tapping. "Good heavens!" she exclaimed. "What's happening?"

"That's called a beat, sister." Rocky grinned. "Feel it pulsing through your body?"

Bunty was now bouncing to the beat. "Yes. Pulsing. Fancy that." She giggled.

"Then, go with it, baby. Go with it!" Rocky encouraged her.

Bunty burst out, moving her body, even adding arm movements. "Look at me! I'm going with it!" she cried.

Babs was alarmed. "Bunty! What's got into you?" she said.

"Same thing that's got into you, apparently!" said Bunty.

Babs looked down. Good grief—now *her* foot was tapping. She started bouncing, then swaying her arms, and soon—she was dancing, too.

And then, everybody was dancing! All the other chickens were bouncing and grooving to the beat.

"Just go with the flow, gals!" said Rocky. He moved amongst them as they got more and more carried away. Now even the chickens sitting in their bunks were doing synchronized hand-jive moves.

Babs was really getting into it now, doing the funky chicken. "Swing it, sister!" said Rocky.

"I'm swinging, I'm swinging!" Babs sang out.

Into this mad scene walked Fowler. He was not amused.

"A dance!" he squawked. "Now, see here! I don't recall authorizing a hop, especially when—"

"Ah, shut up and dance," said Bunty, pulling him onto the floor and swinging him around.

Up in the rafters, Nick and Fetcher had hung a mirrored Christmas ornament. The light ricocheted off it as it spun like a disco ball. Little spots of light wheeled around the room, polka-dotting the dancers as they bounced to the music.

Nick looked over at Fetcher and noticed he was crying. "What are you sobbin' about, y' nancy?" he asked.

"Lit'le moments like this, mate"—his partner sniffled—"it's wot makes the job all worthwhile."

Off to the side of the room, Mac did her own little Scottish clog-dancing moves.

Ginger stood off to the side, watching. Then she got bumped from behind and knocked out into the middle of the dance floor. Chickens were bouncing all around her. She got bumped again, and again, until she was caught by . . . Rocky.

Since he had her on the dance floor, Rocky tried to get her to dance. Ginger resisted. He tried again, and she resisted a little less. Everyone was dancing, stepping in sync, flapping to the right, flapping to the left. And most notably, they were smiling. They were happy. Ginger gave up the fight.

Rocky and Ginger started to dance, tentatively at first. She giggled in a most un-Ginger-like way, and then quickly stifled it. Before long, though, with everyone dancing around them, they were going at it full tilt.

Near the end of the song, they were all dancing in unison. Bunty grabbed Babs and gave her a good twirl. Babs nearly lost her balance, and flapped to steady herself.

But instead of steadying herself, she *flew up onto a top bunk*.

Babs gasped. "Did you see that? I-I-I *flew*!"

The chickens gathered excitedly around her, chattering, congratulating her, and flooding her with questions.

"How did you do it?"

"What did it feel like?"

"How did you get up there?"

Rocky, off to the side with Ginger, clapped both hands and whistled. There was no way he wasn't going to capitalize on the moment. "And *that*," he said, "is why I had this dance." He clapped loudly. "Atta girl, Babsy!" he called.

All of a sudden, Ginger realized something. "Your wing! It's better!" she said to Rocky.

Rocky stopped clapping and looked at his wing. He was busted!

"Um, yeah," he muttered. "Whattaya know about that."

"Fantastic!" said Ginger. "You can *fly* for us tomorrow."

Rocky looked a little sick. "Heh-heh, so it seems," he said with a pained smile.

Ginger swept her wing over the crowd of chickens. "I mean, look at them!" she said. "Imagine how excited they'll be when they see *you* fly around the whole farm."

"Yeah. That'll be something, all right," he mumbled. His mind was racing. The jig was up. Was there any possible way he could get out of being exposed as the total, miserable fraud he was?

Ginger looked at all the smiling chickens, and then back to Rocky.

"I believe I owe you an apology," she said. "I didn't think you cared about us, but after all this, it seems I was wrong."

"Easy, Miss Hard-boiled," said Rocky. "I might think you're turnin' soft."

Suddenly, Ginger and Rocky found themselves staring into each other's eyes."

"Listen, um," Rocky continued, "there's something I gotta tell you."

But before he could speak, he was interrupted by a new and terrifying sound, a deafening rumble.

All the chickens froze.

Ginger listened hard. What could this new sound be?

The lights dimmed, the radio crackled, and the music turned to static.

Pies

A loud engine could now be heard, belching as it fired to life. The chickens held their ears and began to mumble, worried and confused.

Ginger moved toward the door, and Rocky followed. Just before they stepped out of the building, she turned to him.

"You'd better wait here," said Ginger. Rocky nodded and backed away. The other chickens moved to follow Ginger.

The chickens, led by Ginger, filed out of Hut 17. They huddled at the fence to take a closer look. Black smoke was billowing out of the chimney on the roof of the barn.

Inside the barn, Mr. Tweedy was working on the machine he had put together, the one that had come in the big crate. He turned a dial, and the sputtering machine began purring like a Rolls Royce. With some satisfaction he stepped back and watched it run.

"Oh, that's champion, that is," he said to his wife. "Er... what is it?"

She gave him a deadpan stare.

"It's a pie machine, you idiot. Didn't you read the manual?" She turned to look at it. "Chickens go in, pies come out."

"What kind of pies?"

"Apple," said Mrs. Tweedy, her voice dripping with sarcasm.

"My favorite!" exclaimed Mr. Tweedy happily.

Mrs. Tweedy was at the end of her short tether. How much slower could he *be*? "Chicken pies, you stupid git!" She regarded the machine, eyes glimmering. "Imagine it. In less than a fortnight, every grocer's in the county will be stocked with box upon box of Mrs. Tweedy's Homemade Chicken Pies."

"Mrs.?" echoed Mr. Tweedy.

"Woman's touch. Make the public feel more comfortable." Mrs. Tweedy gave a great snort, and then spat on the ground.

"Oh... er, um... how does it work?" Mr. Tweedy wanted to know.

"Get me a chicken and I'll show you," said Mrs. Tweedy, a sinister gleam in her eye.

"I know just the one," replied Mr. Tweedy.

Moments later, Ginger was in deep trouble. She was face to face with a huge, snarling, slobbering dog, so close she could feel his hot breath against her feathers. As he inched forward, Ginger inched backward, not realizing that with every step she was backing closer and closer toward Mr. Tweedy's waiting hand.

Grabbing her roughly, Mr. Tweedy scooped her up and carried her to the barn as the other chickens watched.

"Bloomin' 'eck! He's got Ginger!" clucked Babs.

"We mustn't panic. We mustn't panic!" said Bunty. And she immediately panicked.

Then all the chickens panicked.

"Quiet there," Fowler ordered them over the din. "*Quiet, I say!*"

Rocky poked his head outside the hut, while Fowler kept talking.

"Let's have some discipline, what-what! The enemy has taken a prisoner. This calls for retaliation! Retaliation, I say."

"What's happening? What's going on?" Rocky asked.

"They got Ginger, Mr. Rhodes!" said Babs. "They're taking her to the chop!"

More panic ensued, while Rocky stood there, frozen.

"For Pete's sake, what are you waiting for, lad?" said Fowler. "*Fly* over there, save her!"

Rocky was unable to stifle a small, horrified gasp. "Uh,

right . . . no . . . that's just what the enemy would expect," he said, thinking fast. "But I say we give 'em the um, the um . . . the element of surprise!"

"And catch Jerry with his trousers down," said Fowler, still talking about the Germans as if the Second World War had never ended. "I like the sound of it. What's the plan?"

Rocky scanned the yard. "The plan, the plan, the plan . . ."

He spotted a telegraph pole with an electrical cable running into the upper loft window of the barn. Then, still looking for ideas, he noticed that Babs's knitting bag had a small coat hanger poking out.

Aha.

"Babs, gimme that thing," he said. She handed him the coat hanger.

"Bunty. Gimme a boost."

Bunty complied, lifting Rocky easily to help him reach the wire.

Then they all watched as Rocky hooked the coat hanger onto the wire and slid down toward the open barn window.

He might have been hoping he looked heroic, but actually he looked completely terrified.

"Ahhhhh!" he shrieked as he whizzed down the wire.

Inside the barn, Mr. Tweedy was clamping Ginger's feet into ankle holders on an overhead conveyor belt. He pushed a couple of levers and the belt started moving

Ginger toward the big opening in the machine.

Mr. Tweedy was pleased. "Chickens go in . . . pies come out," he chanted.

The Tweedys now moved around to the side of the machine where the pies would come out.

"Chicken pies," said Mr. Tweedy, concentrating hard. "Not apple. Chicken." He didn't want to make the missus angry again.

Ginger struggled ineffectually against her ankle clamps. Up ahead, she could see that the clamps released just over a large chute that led to who-knew-where.

"Oh, God—help me!" she cried. This was a situation she could not think her way out of, or even will her way out of. She was totally helpless.

At this moment, Rocky popped up behind her. She had never dreamed she would be so happy to see him in her life.

"I'm coming!" he called.

He jumped up and found himself being carried the opposite way on the conveyor belt. "Still coming!" he said, his legs churning madly. More than anything he'd ever done, he wanted to get to Ginger and save her. Beneath her tough exterior, Rocky had a feeling she liked him.

"Stop this thing!" yelled Ginger. "Hurry!"

"I'm getting there," said Rocky, fighting the conveyor belt.

Finally, he made a leap for her, but he was just seconds too late. The ankle clamps released, and Ginger fell down the chute. She was gone from his grasp.

"*Ah!*" she gasped.

"Oh . . . shoot!" said Rocky, making an inadvertent pun as he looked down at her from the top of the chute.

"*Rock-eeeeee!*" screamed the helpless Ginger.

As Rocky looked down to where Ginger had fallen, he was unaware that he was standing on a lever. Since he didn't know he was standing on it, he also didn't know that it was moving downward under his weight. When it reached its lowest point, it turned on an indicator light. The light was labeled Veg Feed.

"I'll be down," he called to Ginger, "before you can say"—he looked above him—"mixed vegetables!" he screamed, for a trough of mixed vegetables was now pouring down on his head, sending him hurtling down the chute.

"Whaaaa . . . ohhhh!" he screeched as he slid.

Ahead of him was a sign that said Mixed Vegetables—This Way. But just before he arrived, it flipped over. Now it read Meat—That Way.

Still zooming downward, Rocky was diverted down another chute that sent him toward a set of—AAAAAAHHH!—*rotating saw blades!* He was going to be minced rooster!

There was almost no time to think. At the last second, Rocky noticed a pole he could reach. He grabbed onto it and slid down, finding himself plummeting down a dark shaft. Down below, he could see that in the depths of the machine was a labyrinth of conveyor belts going in all directions, with huge, noisy stampers and rollers and pushers and clompers going the whole time.

Flump! He landed in a big clump of dough that was chugging along on a conveyor belt. And there, to his surprise and relief, was Ginger, chugging along as well.

"D'oh! Hey, get it? Dough!" quipped Rocky, clowning to cheer her up.

Ginger was in no mood. "We're both gonna get it if we don't get out," she said.

It was true too, because there was another menace ahead of them. It was some sort of a giant roller, rounding the corner and coming down the conveyor belt toward them. They squinted at it, trying to figure out what its purpose was.

In a second, it was clear. It rumbled toward them, flattening all the clumps of dough—squash, squash, squash. In a second, it would flatten them, too.

Rocky struggled mightily to get out of his dough ball, but he was far too mucked up in it. So he hopped, with the dough attached to his feet, over to Ginger. The roller was approaching at a fast clip.

Aha! There was a chain, swinging over the conveyor belt. They jumped for it, grabbing it and holding on, their feet still balled up in dough. As they clung to it for dear life, the chain hoisted them up and out of the way of the dough-roller. They were safe!

But no. No, no, no. They weren't safe at all, because all the chain did was deposit them onto yet *another* conveyor belt.

And what was this they had been plopped down in? Something flat, round, and silver . . . a huge pie tin! A tin for chicken pie!

Before they could figure out what to do next—*fwump!*— a giant stamper slammed down on top of them, squishing them down. As they kept moving, trying to straighten themselves back up again, their tin moved onto yet another belt.

This, apparently, was the part where the diced vegetables came raining down on them. All they could do was duck the carrots, peas, and celery, hoping to be through the veggie storm soon.

And what was this? Some sort of a huge bulbous thing, a new and mystifying horror. It looked like some kind of torture instrument.

Squirt, squirt, squirt. It was a giant gravy dispenser, squirting scalding gravy into the tins in front of them! And they were heading right for it.

They looked around. There was nothing to grab—no pole, no chain, no nothing. They were doomed to death by gravy.

Then, at the last second, Rocky got an idea. He grabbed a carrot and, wielding it like an orange lance, shoved it right smack into the hot snout of the gravy blaster. The carrot plug held. Very quickly, the rubber sacs of the dispenser began to back up and fill with gravy.

"Well. That covers that," said Rocky.

But there was still the top of the pie to contend with. *Splat*—down came a layer of pastry onto them, covering them up.

The Rocky-and-Ginger-pie slid down a ramp, and soon they found themselves in a large room. Other pies were already stacked up on racks, waiting for something.

Rocky and Ginger waited too. At least it was quiet here. Nothing seemed to be coming at them for the moment. It was a place they could rest for a minute.

It was kind of a cozy place. A warm place. A very warm place.

Rocky wiped his brow. "Whoa," he said. "It's like an oven in here."

It was getting hotter by the second. Suddenly blue flames began to light all around them, shooting out of the floor. At the front of the room, a large, heavy door started to close. An oven door. This wasn't just *like* an oven, it *was* an oven!

"And we're the main course. The door! Quickly!" cried Ginger.

She raced for the door, followed by Rocky, who immediately fell into the next pie. His feet were still gummed up in dough.

"Wait up," he called. "I'm com— Whoa, don't leave, I'm . . . blllh . . . Get over to the blah . . ." He was trying to keep up, he really was, but he kept on falling into the pies.

"My savior," said Ginger sardonically, as she watched Rocky stumbling after her.

She dove through the space beneath the lowering door, looking back for Rocky as she did so. He was struggling toward her, having fallen into nearly every pie in the oven. He was covered with gravy.

"C'mon!" Ginger yelled. "Quick!" She grabbed a wrench and stuck it in the door to hold it open. Then she raced back inside, pulled Rocky out of the pie he was mucked up in, and rushed him toward the door. There was no time to lose. The door was now bending the wrench.

Ginger dragged Rocky to the closing door, and they half-leaped, half-rolled through just in the nick of time.

Uh-oh. Ginger felt the top of her head. Her hat, her beloved hat! There it was on the floor, just inside the door. She couldn't leave it behind. Her heart pounding, she reached back in and snatched it right out of the jaws of the closing door.

Thwump! The heavy door closed.

Clang! Out shot the wrench, flying into the gear works nearby.

The machine ground and groaned. The gravy pressure needle climbed fast, pointing to High, way up into the red.

Outside the machine, the Tweedys were sensing that something was very wrong. Sparks and smoke were starting to spew from the machine.

Mrs. Tweedy, of course, turned on Mr. Tweedy at once. "What did you do, you great pudding?" she demanded.

"I didn't do owt!" he protested. "Nothing!"

"Turn it off! TURN IT OFF!" Mrs. Tweedy screeched.

Back inside the machine, the gravy squirter finally spat out the carrot. It shot past the fleeing Rocky and Ginger and jammed into some of the gear cogs. Unable to turn, but still being driven by the powerful motor, the enormous cogs strained and creaked, and finally burst loose. They began to clatter down the ramp after the two terrified chickens.

Rocky and Ginger tore down the ramp as fast as their legs could carry them. The cogs were at their heels now, ready to cut them to ribbons. But when they reached the bottom, just before the cogs overtook them, what should they find but another dangling chain, waiting to save them. Screaming their heads off, they grabbed the chain and swung out, out, out, over a frightening chasm of gears—and finally, up and out of the machine.

At last they landed. They were out of the horrible machinery. They were on top of a pie box.

At once, a giant press came down from overhead. "Ptthh!" It stamped a label onto Rocky's chest. Ginger peeled it off and read it, horrified.

"We've got to tell the others. Come on," she said, scrambling off the box.

Meanwhile, the machine was going completely haywire as Mr. Tweedy haplessly flipped every lever in sight. Nothing happened.

"It's the big button that says *Off*! Mrs. Tweedy yelled at him. Taking matters into her own bony hands, she grabbed the power cord and unplugged it—but not before being blasted with a glob of gravy.

"Look! I fixed it!" said Mr. Tweedy proudly.

By this time his wife was quivering with rage. She picked up a pie and headed toward him.

Poor Mr. Tweedy.

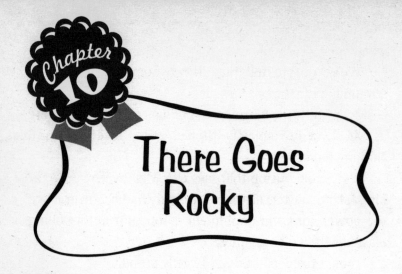

Chapter 10

There Goes Rocky

That night, the chickens gathered in Hut 17. Ginger stood at the head of the group. She was excited. They had met the enemy, and they were going to vanquish it.

Without ceremony, she slapped the pie label onto the wall. It stuck.

"Chicken pies?" said Bunty, bewildered.

"Is that what happens in the barn?" Mac asked.

"Yes, but—" Ginger began, but she was interrupted by a hysterical Babs.

"*I don't want to be a pie!*" Babs bawled. "I don't like gravy!"

The chickens, as they often did in such situations, panicked. Wailing and moaning, they buried their heads in each other's shoulders.

Off to the side, Rocky watched this scene. He was actually feeling sorry for the chickens.

"Ladies, please," Ginger called out over the noise. "Listen. Rocky sabotaged the machine and bought us more time. And better still—he's going to fly for us tomorrow!"

Ginger was so fired up, she didn't notice the figure of Rocky, sidling toward the door.

"And once we've seen how it's done, we'll get it!" Ginger continued. "I know we will. So don't worry, because tomorrow everything is going to go much, much smoother..."

Rocky had quietly left the building. He was now standing just outside the doorway, in the shadows, watching the scene inside. It was easy to read the emotion on his face. He was feeling bad. Feeling responsible. He had led them all on, and now Ginger was pinning all her hopes on something that would never—could never—happen.

He hung his head and walked away.

When he walked into Fowler's hut, he bumped smack into the old rooster, who was standing right there in the doorway.

"Ah!" Rocky gasped. Then he gathered his wits together. "All right, pops. What'd I do now?" he said defensively.

"A very brave and honorable deed, sir," Fowler replied. "I understand that you have saved our Ginger's life."

Rocky was taken aback.

"In light of your actions this evening," Fowler went on, "I dutifully admit that I have misjudged your character. I present you with this medal for bravery..." He pinned a medal onto Rocky's chest. "And I salute you."

Fowler took a step back and gave Rocky a snappy salute.

"In honor of the occasion, I surrender the bunk entirely," he announced. "I shall sleep under the stars." Fowler marched to the door and then turned to Rocky. "I await tomorrow's flying demonstration with great anticipation," he added.

And then, Fowler was gone. Rocky was alone in the bunk. He looked at his medal, and then caught a view of himself in the mirror. He stared at himself, long and hard.

"You and me both, pops," he said under his breath. He left the hut and climbed onto a nearby roof to look at the stars.

Ginger came upon him a few minutes later, sitting up on the roof of her hut in the moonlight. He was staring past his medal, out toward the horizon.

"I'm sorry," said Ginger. "Were you . . . ?"

"Is this your . . . I'll get down." Rocky started to climb off the roof.

"No, no," she said quickly. "It's just . . ."

There was a pause, and then they both started speaking at the same time.

"Well, since you're here, there's something—" Ginger began.

Rocky was speaking too. "I'm glad you're here because I really think I should tell you—"

They both stopped.

"I'm sorry, you go first," said Ginger.

"You go ahead, I'll—" said Rocky at the same time.

They both giggled. It was the first time they had actually laughed together.

Ginger took a breath. "I just wanted to say," she said, "I may have been a bit harsh at first. . . . Well what I really mean is . . . thank you. For saving my life." She looked out toward the hill. "For saving *our* lives," she added.

Rocky gulped.

"You know," Ginger went on, "I come up here every night and look out to that hill and just imagine what it must be like on the other side. I've never felt grass under my feet. I was born in a chicken yard, penned up, with dirt to scratch about in—not even a tree to give us shade, or the cool feeling of raindrops on . . ." She turned to him, suddenly interrupting herself. "I'm sorry. Here I am rambling on about hills and grass, and you had something you wanted to say."

Rocky looked at her for a long moment, and then followed her gaze out to the hill. They were quiet.

"Yeah, well um," he said at last, "it's just that, you know . . . life, as I've experienced it, you know—out there, lone free ranging and stuff—it's full of disappointments."

"You mean, grass isn't all it's cracked up to be?"

"Grass. Exactly. It's always greener on the other side. And then you get there and, and, and it's brown and prickly, you know what I mean?"

Ginger nodded—and then shook her head. She actually had no idea what he meant.

Rocky tried again. "What I'm trying to say is . . ."

He lost the train of his thought, because suddenly he was looking deep into her eyes, feeling things he had never felt in his life.

"You're welcome," he finally said simply.

She smiled, and turned back toward the hill. "That hill is looking closer tonight than it ever has before," she said softly.

She put her hands down to steady herself, and found that she'd accidentally set her hand on his.

Their eyes met for a brief second. Then they nervously pulled their hands apart.

There was an awkward pause.

"Well. Good night . . . Rocky," said Ginger.

She stood to leave.

"Good night . . . Ginger," he said reluctantly.

Ginger smiled. This was the first time he'd ever called her by name.

Then she left.

Rocky looked down to find that one of her feathers was left beside him. He picked it up, looked at it, and looked at the medal he still held in the other hand. Then he pulled out a torn piece of paper. He unfolded it, stared at it for a while, and finally heaved a deep sigh.

"Good night," he said softly.

"Company! COCK-A-DOODLE-DOOOO, WHAT-WHAT!"

It was Fowler, doing his roosterly duty, waking up the hens.

The chickens slowly began coming to life. But when they made their way out of their huts, they found that Ginger was already busy. She was energetically putting up the circus flyer with Rocky's picture, hammering in a nail with a rock.

The hens eagerly surrounded Ginger. She was excited too.

"Today's the day," she announced. "We're going to fly, I can *feel* it."

There were murmurs of enthusiasm from the group.

"Better start warming up," said Ginger. "I'll go get him."

She headed across the compound with a new spring in her step. When she reached Fowler's hut, she knocked on the door.

"Rocky?" she called.

There was no answer from inside. She opened the door a crack and stuck her head inside.

"Knock, knock," she called again. "Coming in. Everyone's waiting, so I told them to—"

Ginger stopped, shocked. The room was empty. Her

heart dropped to her feet.

"Rocky?" she said in a shaky voice.

Looking around the room, her eyes lit upon the torn piece of paper on the bed. It was the paper Rocky had held in his hands the night before. Sitting on top of the paper was the medal.

She walked toward the bed, fearing the worst, picked up the paper, and stared at it in disbelief.

"Oh no," she said, very quietly.

Shoulders hunched, dragging her feet, she walked back to where the hens were waiting. Slowly, she raised the bottom half of the poster, matching it to the top half, which was hanging up.

It was the bottom half of the poster that she had found on Rocky's bed.

And on it was a picture of a cannon—the cannon out of which Rocky had been fired.

There was a lightning flash and a thunderclap, and then a gasp from the chickens. Then, as the rain began to fall, they started to murmur.

Ginger, lifeless and speechless, turned and stared at the chickens. She could not think of a word to say. Finally she plopped down on the ramp into Hut 17 and stared at the ground. She was totally depressed.

At that moment, Rocky was standing on the crest of a

hill on the road outside the farm. He was looking back at the farm. Guilt was not a feeling he was used to having, but he was sure having it now.

After a while, he sighed wistfully, hung his head in shame, and continued walking down the long stretch of road—alone.

Chapter 11

Eggs for Industry, Eggs for Defense

Fowler stood outside Hut 17, staring at the poster. In his hand was the medal Rocky had left behind. He looked grave. "Desertion. A report I shan't enjoy filing," he said to himself.

The chickens were still huddled around the poster. They were too shocked, stunned, and dumbfounded to move.

"A cannon," said Mac, shaking her head. "Aye, that'll give you throost."

Bunty was irate. "I knew he was a fake all along," she said. "In fact, I'm not even certain he was American."

Mac turned to Ginger. "So, what's the next plan, hen?" she asked

Ginger sat with her back to them. "Let's face it," she said without turning around. "The only way out of here—is wrapped in pastry."

The hens shuffled nervously at the thought.

Babs raised her hand. She was still working on the problem of what had happened to Rocky. "Perhaps he just went on holiday," she offered.

Bunty turned on her in helpless fury. "P'raps he just went to get away from your infernal knitting!" She grabbed Babs's knitting and threw it on the ground.

"You were the one always hittin' him!" Mac burst out. "See how you like it!" She smacked Bunty on the back, hard.

"Don't push me, four-eyes!" Bunty warned, pushing Mac with her back.

Mac lost her balance and fell down in the mud. She picked up a handful of mud and flung it at Bunty.

Bunty ducked. *Splat!* The mud hit Babs.

And then, all bedlam broke loose. The chickens erupted into a full-fledged mud fight. Mud was flying in all directions through the air, hens were sliding into each other, everything was a great big muddy mess.

In the middle of it all, Fowler stepped into the fray.

"Quiet there! *Quiet I say!*" he shouted.

The chickens froze in midfight. What were they *doing*? They bowed their heads, ashamed.

"Dissension in the ranks, precisely what Jerry would've wanted," barked Fowler, pacing up and down before the mud-spattered crowd. "The old divide and conquer!" Now he was really cranking himself up to a full-scale tirade. "No! A proper squadron must work together! Just like we did in my RAF days. With Jocko at the stick, Flappy at the map, and old Whizzbang the tail end Charlie. Wingco would give the call—'Tallyho! Bandits at three o'clock!' And it's 'Pull your finger out, boys, and get weaving!' Hop in the old crate and chocks away! Wizard show it was." He held out his medal for all to see. "That's why the RAF gave you medals!"

"Will you shut up about your stupid bloomin' medals?" Bunty said, swatting the medal out of his hand.

It flew through the air, tumbling over and over. Finally it thunked Ginger in the head, bounced off, and splashed into a puddle.

"How *dare* you!" Fowler sputtered. Then he thwacked Bunty on the head with his walking stick.

There was silence.

Fowler suddenly returned to his senses, mortified. "Madame. Forgive me," he said. "As an officer, I offer my most sincere—"

Smack! Bunty's fist connected with Fowler's beak.

The mud fight resumed at full tilt.

But Ginger was not slinging mud. In the middle of the chaos, Ginger was having a thoughtful moment. She reached down, picked up the medal, and stared at it. Then she wiped some mud off it, revealing the letters . . . RAF

Ginger looked puzzled. "Fowler?" she said.

She straightened up and turned around, only to notice

the mud fight that was going in full force behind her.

She took a deep breath. "Fowler!?" she said loudly.

Nobody paid any attention.

She took a deeper breath. "EVERYONE! SHUT UP!" she yelled at the top of her lungs.

That worked. The chickens froze in midpunch and midswipe, and turned to face Ginger. Suddenly it was quiet.

"Fowler?" said Ginger slowly. "What exactly *is*—the RAF?"

"What do you mean, what is it?" Fowler said. "The Royal Air Force is what, what-what."

"Air force?" Ginger repeated.

She gazed at the medal some more.

"If it's the *air* force, then—what's 'the old crate' you're always talking about?" she asked him.

Fowler drew himself up, looking as proud as an old military rooster can look.

Minutes later, Fowler was in his hut with Ginger and the others. He opened his footlocker. With loving carefulness, he pulled out a photograph and showed it to Ginger. "Gorgeous, isn't she?" he said. "And beautifully built."

Ginger was confused. "You mean you *flew*? In one of *these*?"

Fowler was happy to launch into a long-winded explanation. "In fact, there's a bit of a story to that as well," he began. "We were out on a mission, you see. Ops had given us the go-ahead..."

Fowler went on and on, but Ginger was not with him. Ginger was getting an idea.

"...but the weather duffed up," Fowler was saying excitedly. "Frightful wind. Right over the white cliffs of Dover. Nearly ditched the old girl in the drink. Would have been a fearful prang, but old Jocko held her steady. He was a keen type, old Jocko. Bang on. Wizard show. Wizard show!"

"It's perfect!" Ginger suddenly exclaimed, interrupting Fowler. "Absolutely perfect!"

The chickens were in their usual state of babbling muddleheadedness.

"Perfect?"

"What's perfect?"

"What is she talking about?"

Ginger now leaped up onto the footlocker, filled with new hope. "We're still going to fly out of here!" she announced. "Fowler's provided the answer."

Fowler didn't understand, but he was nonetheless pleased as punch. "I have? Yes, yes—of course I have. Er, um... how have I?"

Ginger dramatically turned the photo around so everyone could see it. The photo was of a World War II Royal Air Force bomber airplane.

"We'll make," she said, "a crate."

Suddenly, the chicken yard was electric with excitement and activity.

Fowler unloaded an armful of old RAF photographs onto a table for everyone's reference.

Mac sat at a makeshift drafting table, furiously sketching out blueprints.

"Mac, you'll handle the engineering," Ginger told her.

Babs was showing three other chickens how to knit and stitch.

"Babs—manufacturing," said Ginger. "Fowler will be chief aviation adviser."

She then opened the door, letting out Agnes, who ran over toward the fence, waving her arms and clucking wildly. On the other side of the fence, the dogs barked and rushed at her. Agnes ran along the fence one way, and the dogs followed. She ran the other way, and the dogs followed, wild to get through the chain link. Fortunately, the fence was strong enough to keep the dogs out. Meanwhile, in another part of the yard, another chicken was scurrying toward Hut 17, carrying an armful of various and sundry supplies.

"Agnes—diversions," said Ginger.

"Bunty," Ginger went on. "Eggs."

Bunty, who hadn't been around for the previous assignment of jobs, stopped in midstride. She looked confused.

"Eggs?" she said.

✄ ✄ ✄ ✄

"Eggs," said Nick, looking right at Ginger a bit later. He and Fetcher were having a business meeting with Ginger and Bunty.

"Right," Nick said, "just like the ones that rooster was gonna lay. Only roosters don't lay eggs, do they?"

"Don't they?" said Fetcher.

"It's a lady thing," Nick explained to him. "Ask your mum."

Ginger held her list, all business. "One egg for every item on the list," she said curtly. "First payment in advance." She placed one of Bunty's eggs in Nick's hand.

"Right," said Nick, trying to look blasé. "When do we start?"

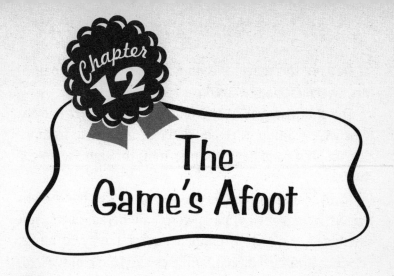

The Game's Afoot

Mr. Tweedy was trying to start up the pie machine, as his wife hovered behind him. The machine ground, groaned, almost started—and then sputtered out.

Mrs. Tweedy smacked Mr. Tweedy on the head and stalked out of the barn.

A moment later, two garden gnomes, complete with tiny garden tools, scooted into the barn and stopped beside Mr. Tweedy's screwdriver.

One of the gnomes lifted slightly of the ground, and out darted two rat hands. Quick as a wink, they swiped the screwdriver and yanked it inside the gnome. Then the gnomes scooted away.

Mr. Tweedy looked up just in time to see the gnomes scurrying away. His screwdriver was gone. "What the dickens?" he said, rubbing his eyes. Then he shrugged, resigned. "Oh, gnomes now."

Outside the fence, the dogs were sleeping. A pair of Mrs. Tweedy's shoes walked past them—empty.

The shoes arrived at the fence, where Ginger and the hens were waiting. Nick and Fetcher popped up from inside the shoes and began to pass tools through the hole in the fence.

In the chicken hut, serious construction had begun. Screws were screwed, nails were hammered, parts were assembled, nails were popped out of huts and bunks, everybody on the chicken farm was busy, busy, busy.

In the barn, Mr. Tweedy tried to start the machine again. It chugged and churned and finally sputtered off.

The rats ran back and forth across the yard, bringing more and more tools and supplies, as the chickens sewed, cut fabric, and kept working on the crate.

Bunty, meanwhile, was producing the eggs that were necessary to keep the whole enterprise going. She just kept laying and laying and laying. As she turned a hand drill for the construction, an egg came out with every turn.

The eggs fell gently into a waiting carton, which was tended by the salivating Nick and Fetcher.

"Eggs from heaven!" said Nick.

"No, from the bum!" Fetcher corrected him.

As the frantic sawing, hammering, and tying continued, so did Mr. Tweedy's efforts to start up the machine. Once, he actually got it to start up, as Mrs. Tweedy stood behind him, glaring. The machine chugged for a moment and then died again. Mrs. Tweedy gave her husband a swift kick in the rear.

Ginger looked nervously out the window of the hut, toward the barn. "That was close," she said to her troops. "Too close. Come on, everyone. Keep at it, we're nearly there. Go, go, go, go, go."

She walked among them, feeling proud of the amazing enterprise they had pulled together out of nothing. "Agnes," she said, double-check those fittings. Mac, we need those calculations—quickly! Steady up there, Fowler! Bunty, give him a hand! We can do this, we can do it. Babs, great work!"

"No problem, doll face!" Babs called back.

The other chickens laughed, and Ginger smiled, too. Then, all at once, her smile faded as it suddenly hit her: She actually *missed* that big dope calling her doll face. She missed Rocky.

She walked out of the hut, past the circus poster that was still clinging to the wall.

Where had he gone?

At that moment, Rocky was out in the world, riding along on a tricycle.

Pretty soon he pedaled past a large billboard. "Mrs. Tweedy's Chicken Pies," it read. Mrs. Tweedy's face was all made up on the billboard. She looked very charming indeed in her gingham apron. Only those who knew her would notice that sinister something lurking behind her little smile. Rocky passed by the billboard. Then, a moment later, he pedaled backward and stopped in front of it. He looked at the green grass beneath it. Then he looked behind him. He could see Tweedy's Farm, way down in the valley.

He bowed his head and sighed.

The real Mrs. Tweedy, at that moment, was not looking a bit charming. She was staring daggers at Mr. Tweedy, as usual. "I thought you said you fixed it!" she yelled.

Mr. Tweedy turned the ignition. The machine made grinding and sputtering sounds.

"I did!" said Mr. Tweedy. He gave the machine a little kick. "C'mon, c'mon," he said under his breath.

The machine coughed some more, and then—*gr-grr-grrrr*—it started up.

In Hut 17, the chickens heard the machine running. They all froze.

"Oh no!" cried Ginger.

Mrs. Tweedy smiled with delight as she watched the machine. "Get the chickens," she ordered.

"Which one?" Mr. Tweedy asked her.

She turned the machine up full blast. "All of them!" she replied.

Listening to the machine, the hens were starting to panic. Mac looked to Ginger, as always, for leadership. "What's the plan, hen?" she said.

Before Ginger could answer—*blam!* The door slammed open and Mr. Tweedy shoved his head inside. His eyes widened at the sight of the huge construction operation in Hut 17.

If Ginger didn't think fast, all would be lost. She made her decision in a split second.

"*Attack!*" she yelled.

Leading the charge, she sprang onto Mr. Tweedy's face. The other chickens followed suit. One latched onto his nose, another onto his ear. They were all over him, on his shoulders, his arms, his legs. Screaming, he backed out of the hut.

Mrs. Tweedy, in the meantime, was in the barn adding up figures on a note pad and talking to herself. "Let's see.... If I charge two pounds a pie times four hundred pies... carry the two..."

If she had cared to look through the window, she might have seen Mr. Tweedy backing into the yard, covered from head to toe with chickens.

"Mrs. Tweedy!" he screamed. "*The chickens are revolting!*"

Mrs. Tweedy did not look up from her figures, and so it

did not occur to her that her husband was using a quite different meaning of the word from the one she had in mind. "Finally, something we agree on," she said without much interest.

Her husband stumbled around, flailing and thrashing, then fell out of view just as Mrs. Tweedy turned around. She looked across the yard, furrowing her brow. Nothing.

Then she checked her watch and went back to her figures.

In the compound, the chickens bound Mr. Tweedy with twine and shoved him unceremoniously under a hut. "Nice plan," Mac said to Ginger with satisfaction.

Bunty shoved Mr. Tweedy's cap in his mouth, gagging him. "See how you like bein' stuffed!" she said.

The dogs continued to bark outside the fence. Mr. Tweedy flailed and struggled, his eyes bulging.

Babs suddenly gave in to panic. "What have we done?" she blithered. "Mrs. Farmer will find him and kill us all!"

"We won't be around," said Ginger firmly. "Everyone into position. We're escaping—now!"

There was low-grade panic among the chicken population, but Ginger was resolute. "We'll either die free chickens," she said, "or die trying."

There was a minute of silence as everybody tried to figure that out.

"Are those the only choices?" Babs asked at last. She received a silencing stare from the others.

Ginger turned to her chief technical adviser. "Fowler . . . ?" she said.

Fowler snapped to it. "*Scramble!*" he ordered.

Under cover of night, the chickens secretively scampered into their designated positions. Some of them manned ropes, others readied themselves behind huts awaiting Ginger's command.

"Now!" whispered Ginger loudly.

Ropes were pulled, cranks cranked, levers deployed. A ramp was lifted up near the fence. There were arrows drawn on it, pointing upward. And on it were painted the words This Way Up.

Down the path between the huts, a pair of chickens uncoiled two rows of Christmas lights, creating a dandy lighted runway.

And then magically, dramatically, from Hut 17 and its surrounding huts emerged a giant wooden airplane.

Mr. Tweedy, still bound, watched from beneath the hut.

"Rhzzziz Reeewry!" he exclaimed through his hat, which was still shoved into his mouth.

In the barn, Mrs. Tweedy turned. Had she heard something?

Inside the flying machine, Nick and Fetcher had already found something to do. "Kindly direct your attention to the front of the aircraft for a few safety instructions," Nick said smoothly, gesturing broadly like a flight attendant. "The exits are located *here* and *here*. In the quite *likely* event of an emergency, put your head between your knees and—"

"Kiss your bum good-bye," Fetcher finished.

Ginger entered the flying machine, admiring the great accomplishment that all of them had achieved. She walked up the aisle toward the cockpit.

"All right, Fowler!" she sang out. "We're ready for take-off."

"Behind you all the way!" said Fowler.

Ginger spun around. To her total shock, Fowler was seated right beside her. *Behind* the pilot's seat!

"You're supposed to be up there," Ginger said to him, pointing to the cockpit. "*You're* the pilot."

"Don't be ridiculous," he replied. "I can't fly this contraption."

This caused the confused, worried, chicken-murmuring thing to start up—big time.

Ginger was also confused and worried. "But . . . back in your day. Th-the Royal Air Force . . ."

"Six hundred forty-fourth Squadron, poultry division," Fowler said proudly. "We were the mascots."

More murmurs from the group.

"What?"

"What did he say?"

Ginger could not believe what she'd just heard. "The *mascot*? You mean, you never *flew* the plane?"

"Good heavens, no!" Fowler chuckled. "I'm a *chicken*. The Royal Air Force didn't let chickens behind the controls of a complex aircraft."

Ginger turned to Fowler, determination on her face. "Fowler, listen to me," she said. "You *have* to fly it."

"But—" he protested.

"You're always talking about 'back in your day,'" Ginger said. "Well, *today* is your day."

With great gravity, Ginger pinned the RAF medal to his chest. He looked at it, and then looked uncertainly at the other hens. They all returned him a nod of confidence. He looked at Ginger. She nodded too.

"You can do it . . . sausage!" said Bunty with a wink.

That did it. Fowler swelled with pride, puffed up his chest, and snapped into a full salute. "Wing Commander T. I. Fowler, reporting for duty!" he crowed.

Ginger saluted back.

"Well, come on, what are you waiting for? We haven't got all day. Let's get this crate off the ground!"

"Fowler, *now!*" cried Ginger in exasperation.

Fowler climbed the ladder up into the cockpit, looked at his medal, and nodded.

"Roger!" he said, manipulating the levers.

He picked up a tin can with a string tied to it, a

makeshift two-way radio. "Contact!" he reported.

Farther back in the plane, several chickens now began pedaling madly. The pedals caused a set of gears to turn— which in turn started the propeller turning.

Fowler looked down the lit runway toward the This Way Up ramp. "Clear for takeoff! Full throttle!" he said into his radio.

The chickens pedaled faster, starting a set of giant gears turning. Not only did the propeller spin faster, but *the wings began to flap*. It looked like a huge bird of prey.

"Chocks away!" Fowler yelled.

Pulling on two ropes, the chickens removed the wooden blocks that kept the contraption from rolling away.

The plane inched forward. It lurched down the runway, picking up speed as it got closer and closer to the ramp. It moved past Mr. Tweedy, who was still under the hut, but slowly edging his way out.

Ginger joined Fowler in the cockpit, anxiously looking out the front window as the plane got nearer and nearer to the ramp.

"We need more power!" called Fowler.

"I cannot work miracles, cap'n. We're giving her all she's got!" Mac called back in her Scottish accent.

And then, suddenly . . . *disaster*. Just before they got to the ramp, Mr. Tweedy leaped out in front of the plane. He was still bound, but he was able to kick the ramp down.

"Gotcha!" he cried.

Fowler panicked. "Hard right!" he yelled back to Mac.

The right row of chickens backpedaled, and the left row pedaled faster, turning the plane the way oarsmen turn a boat.

It worked like a charm. The plane made a hard right, knocking Mr. Tweedy to the ground.

The plane kept bumping and clunking along, but now it was going in the wrong direction.

"Turn it around. I'll get the ramp!" Ginger cried.

Meanwhile, the chickens turned the plane around. But now the Christmas lights on the runway were tangled up in the rear wheel (which was actually a paint roller).

Ginger had reached the ramp and begun the struggle to push it up into position again.

All of a sudden—*thwack!*—an ax slammed into the ramp, a hairsbreadth from Ginger's head.

Ginger looked up. There was Mrs. Tweedy, heaving mightily on the ax to remove it and strike again.

This was it, this was the end of the line. Ginger was doomed, they were all doomed.

"*Gingerrrrr!*"

She looked up. What was that voice, wafting toward her at the moment of her death? She knew that voice.

That was Rocky's voice.

And there he was, speeding downhill on his tricycle.

Rocky Rhodes, daredevil extraordinaire, coming back to help his friends!

"Heads up!" he yelled.

He aimed for a large mound of dirt just before the barbed-wire fence. *Boink!* He hit it hard, went sailing into the air, cleared the fence, and kept going.

Mrs. Tweedy looked up—just as the front tire of the trike conked her on the forehead and sent her sprawling. She fell backward, and the ax fell to the ground, pinning her by her hair.

Rocky landed in front of Ginger. Very coolly, he skidded the trike to a sideways stop and thumbed the bell on the handlebars, as if he were revving the engine.

It was cute, very cute, but there was no time for reunions. The plane was headed right for them.

"Clear the runway, Yank!" Fowler shouted from the plane.

"Help me!" Ginger cried. "*The ramp!* Quickly!"

They both grabbed the heavy ramp and started working feverishly to hoist it up onto the fence as the plane rumbled closer and closer. There! It was up! With not a moment to spare, they managed to wedge the wooden brace into place and roll out of the way just as the wheels of the plane hit the ramp.

The plane rolled up it and soared over the fence to freedom.

But what were Rocky and Ginger going to do? They were still inside the farm!

And then the answer came to them, dangling above their heads. The Christmas lights! They were still dragging behind the plane, caught in the axle.

"Grab on!" Rocky yelled.

Rocky and Ginger grabbed on to the string of lights, held on tight, and soared up into the air. They were out!

Hanging on to the lights for dear life, inching along, they managed to climb on board the plane.

They were safe. They were alone. They were . . . staring into each other's eyes. They stayed this way for a long moment, and then Rocky came closer to Ginger, and closer, and . . .

Smack! She slapped him across the face. "That's for leaving," she said. And then she grabbed him. "And this is for coming back." And she leaned in for a kiss.

Suddenly the plane gave a great jerk. Ginger and Rocky looked back, to see—*aaacckk!*—Mrs. Tweedy was hanging from the Christmas lights! And she was still wielding her ax, grunting as she tried to swing it!

"Oh no! She's grabbed on!" cried Ginger.

Fowler called back from the cockpit. "What was that?"

"A cling-on, Cap'n!" Mac reported. "And the engines can't take it!"

Ginger looked down to see the lights still tangled in the plane's rear axle. "We need something to cut her loose!" she yelled to the chickens.

Babs rifled through her knitting bag, looking for something Ginger could use. Comb? No. Needles? Thread? No.

"Bingo," she said finally, coming up with a pair of scissors. She passed them from chicken to chicken, until they arrived in Ginger's hands.

"Lower me down!" Ginger said to Rocky.

"What?!" said Rocky. "No way! *I'll* go!"

"I can't hold *you*," Ginger replied.

"But, Ginger..." Rocky protested. But he knew she was right.

"Just do it!" she said, turning toward the door.

Meanwhile, Mrs. Tweedy had put the ax into her mouth and was climbing the Christmas lights toward the plane.

Up above, Ginger put the scissors into *her* mouth and leaned out the back of the plane. Rocky lowered her carefully, holding her by the feet.

Ginger tried to reach the Christmas lights with the scissors, but could not quite make it. "*Lower!*" she shouted to Rocky.

Mrs. Tweedy was still climbing.

The plane jerked downward, as Fowler struggled with the controls. "We're losing altitude!" he called to his crew over the tin-can radio. "Increase velocity!"

"What does that mean?" Babs asked.

"It means pedal your flippin' giblets out!" Bunty yelled. The chickens responded valiantly, their feet a blur of motion.

Ginger, meantime, was still reaching for the strand of lights, trying to cut it, when she happened to notice that they were headed straight for . . . *the billboard for Mrs. Tweedy's Chicken Pies!*

"Fowler! Look out!" she shrieked.

"Great Scott!" Fowler cried. He pulled hard on the stick, and the plane swooped sharply upward.

Dangling from the lights, Mrs. Tweedy smacked hard into the billboard, ripping off the painted image of her own face.

The plane rocked from the impact, and Ginger slipped out of Rocky's grasp. As she fell, she grabbed the wire.

The plane was now whipping out of control.

"Ahhhh!" screamed the chickens, as the plane rocked.

"AHHHHH!" screamed Nick and Fetcher even louder, watching their precious eggs spilling out of their bag.

Hanging on for dear life, Ginger clutched the wire as she slid down it, Christmas lights popping as she went.

Eeeeeeek! Suddenly she was face to face with Mrs. Tweedy's gigantic, painted mug.

The wind whipped the painted picture away, revealing—EEEEEEEEEKKK! Mrs. Tweedy beneath it, rearing back to swing her ax at Ginger!

Suddenly . . . *splat!* An egg hit the horrible woman right in the face.

"Huh?" said Ginger in surprise.

She looked up, and there was Rocky sitting by the catapult they'd used for training. He was firing eggs at Mrs. Tweedy from it.

"Load me!" he barked.

In tears, Nick and Fetcher loaded more of their precious eggs into the catapult.

"Fire!" ordered Rocky.

He fired again, and yet again, ignoring the miserable wails of the rats.

Ginger had to seize this moment. She grasped the scissors firmly and tried with all her might to cut the wire. But they were too small and too dull. They would not go through.

Mrs. Tweedy took another swipe with the ax, knocking the scissors out of Ginger's hand. The went tumbling, end over end, through the air.

Desperate, Ginger tried biting through the wire. It was useless.

As the chickens continued to pedal their hearts out, Mrs. Tweedy climbed another notch toward Ginger. She raised the ax again, aiming it right for Ginger's neck.

"Ginger! *Look out!*" cried Rocky in alarm.

Ginger looked up to see Mrs. Tweedy raising the ax. There was no place to go. **She** was going to get it. Well, it had been a good attempt. Better to die trying than not to try at all. She rested her cheek on the wire, waiting for the chop. She was tired.

And then, just as the ax was almost upon her . . . Ginger got an idea.

Quick as a wink, she held out the wire. *Whack!* The ax sliced cleanly through it.

Mrs. Tweedy looked stunned for a moment, registering what had just happened. Above her, Ginger held the two ends of wire.

Ginger smiled.

"Bye-bye," said Ginger. Then she let one end go and watched the evil Mrs. Tweedy fall, fall, fall . . .

They were now swooping over the barn. Mrs. Tweedy plummeted neatly through the open window at the peak of the barn roof, and fell into the chute of—*the pie machine.*

Immediately, alarms began sounding in the great machine as pressure gauges started rising.

Mr. Tweedy hopped over to the barn door and opened it. "Mrs. Tweedy! MRS. TWEEDY!" he cried as he saw that she was stuck in the machine, and that the machine was just about to blow.

He winced. Then he quietly closed the barn door.

On the airplane, Rocky and Ginger were hugging ecstatically. Rocky leaned in and gave Ginger a kiss. Suddenly, they heard a huge explosion down below: *WHA-BOOOM!* They all looked down, and then flinched as the pie machine exploded behind them, spewing a mushroom cloud of gravy high into the air.

Down below, Mr. Tweedy stood outside the barn door, still wincing from the explosion. He opened the door. The pie machine had been blown to smithereens, and all that was left of it was the exhaust pipe, in which Mrs. Tweedy was stuck. The dogs were eagerly lapping up puddles of gravy around her.

"I told you they was organized," Mr. Tweedy said with satisfaction.

"Ughhhh," said Mrs. Tweedy, closing her eyes.

On the plane, the chickens had erupted into wild cheers. It was time to celebrate!

"Mission accomplished, men!" crowed Fowler.

"Yeaaaahhhhhh!!!" the chickens cheered . . . and stopped pedaling.

Instantly, the plane took a dive.

"We're not there yet!" Fowler reminded them. "Keep pedaling!"

"Ohhhh!" said the chickens.

The plane rose again, and sailed off toward the sunset.

A pair of feet chicken feet curled into the soft green grass. They were Ginger's feet; she was enjoying the feeling of grass for the very first time.

Rocky joined her on the grass. "Is it as good as you imagined?" he asked her.

"Better," she said, grabbing his hand.

The chickens were safe. They ran through the grass, lounged under shade trees, played cricket.

Free.

Nearby, Nick and Fetcher were sitting on a sign. Bird Sanctuary, it read. Keep Out. The word *Bird* had been crossed out and replaced with the word *Chicken*.

Their new paradise was an island in the middle of a tranquil lake. There were no farmers, no dogs, no huts or coops or keys. And no fences.

"Our *own* chicken farm, mate," Nick was rhapsodizing. "That way we'd have eggs when and where we want."

"Right," said Fetcher. "We'll need a chicken then."

"No—we'll need an egg. You have the egg first. That's where you get the chicken from," Nick explained.

"That's crazy talk. If you don't have a chicken, where you gonna get a egg?"

"From the chicken that comes *from* the egg."

"Hang on," said Fetcher. "Let's go over this again."

"Aren't you listening?"

"What about the first turtle, then?"

"The first turtle? What does he have to do with all this?" Nick said.

"Well, turtles come from eggs. And snakes . . . And, what's that funny-looking creature—got a beak—looks a bit like a duck?"

"A platypus?" offered Nick.

"No. Erm . . . a duck, that's it."

"Listen, mate, tell you what. Here's what we're gonna do. From now on, if you think you're going to say something stupid, just don't speak. Right?"

"When do we start then?"

"Now."

"All right. I got something."

"Good. Now don't say it."

And they continued in this vein, as the sun went down over the beautiful green land that was far, far away from Tweedy's Chicken Farm.